TIGER AND THE UNICORN

A FUC ACADEMY STORY

SUSAN HAYES

INTRODUCTION

Forget the wrong side of the tracks. These two shifters are from opposite sides of the food chain.

Sergei is a tiger-shifter who lives by a set of rules as clear as the stripes on his fur. Steaks should always be served rare, catnaps are the best naps, and prey should never try to be predators.

Tabitha was a horse-shifter with a love for lists and a yen for a little adventure. Then she ate the wrong vegan doughnut and woke up with a new hairdo, a horn, and some serious anger management issues. If this is what adventure is like, she's ready to go back to being boring.

He's been hired to train shifters in the art of survival.

She's just trying to get a handle on her new reality.

When destiny throws a librarian and a TV star together,

tempers will flare, passion will burn, and someone's going to get horny.

Does this premise and world seem familiar? That's because it is based off the Eve Langlais Furry United Coalition. Eve Langlais has invited her author friends to come and play in her world. To find out more, visit Worlds.EveLanglais.com.

DEDICATION

To my parents for believing in me no matter how crazy I
sounded.

To Chrysta S. (She knows why)

And to Eve, who is all the best kinds of crazy – Thank you
for inviting me to play in the FUC world!

Sergei needed a hot shower, a rare steak, and twelve hours of uninterrupted sleep. It had been a long week, and there wasn't much time for quality catnaps out in the wild.

It would be a while before any of that would happen, though. So, he indulged in a back-cracking stretch as he watched the agents he'd been training stagger off the bus.

All in all, they'd been an impressive lot, but the Furry United Coalition only hired the best shifters to be agents. All of them dedicated to protecting their own from all sorts of threats, especially the human variety. He should know, he'd been one of them, once.

The FUC agents on this trip had all been top-notch, with one notable exception. He was the last to limp off the bus. He wobbled on long, unsteady legs, thin shoulders slumped, head hanging down in dejected defeat.

"Chin up, Flavio, at least you didn't die," Sergei called out.

The man groaned. "Now I know why all those other birds fly south for the winter. Snow sucks."

Flavio was a member of ASS - Avian Soaring Security. They were the bird shifter's version of FUC, and they had to be run by feather-brained fools. Why else would they recruit their smaller, more delicate shifters to work as field agents? Prey animals had skills and abilities that could be used by FUC, ASS, and other agencies, sure. But what could a pigeon do in a fight against a wolf or a bear? Other than make serving suggestions like ' I'd taste best with a bit of lemon and a hint of tarragon,' and 'please, kill me quickly.'

Surviving in the wild wasn't just a physical challenge, it was a mental one, and Flavio simply didn't have what it took. Still, he wasn't entirely to blame for his poor performance. The bird knew his limits, even if his superiors hadn't. Why else would they send a fucking *flamingo* for survival training to the Canadian Rocky Mountains in late winter?

The group headed for the academy's main building, no doubt to find hot food and a warm bed.

Sergei stood still and watched them go. As much as he wanted to join them, he had an image to uphold. He was Sergei Molotov - tiger shifter, retired FUC agent, survivalist trainer, and the star of the hit television show, *Survive This!* He wasn't affected by weather, natural disasters, or anything else Mother Nature threw at him.

He lingered outside until he was alone. Well, almost alone. Despite the growing darkness and sleet, he caught a flash of movement on the obstacle course.

He hadn't shifted to his tiger form in days. He was more than a little tempted to go furry and give chase, especially once he took a better look and realized the runner was a very shapely female. Long legs, nice ass, and the perfect amount of curves to put a bounce into more than her step. *Yummy.* He was a predator, after all—chasing down tasty morsels was in his DNA.

He drew in a deep breath, trying to pick out her scent. He could usually tell a lot about someone that way. Shifter type, diet, arousal level—all sorts of interesting information. Not today, though. The rain and cold ran interference. All he could be sure of was that she was healthy and female, and his eyes had told him that much already.

She had to be either a cadet or an instructor. Not that it mattered much. FUCN'A, the Furry United Coalition Newbie Academy, might have rules about fraternizing between cadets and instructors, but he was a freelancer, and the sessions he ran didn't have grades.

The lone runner flew through the first few obstacles, but she hesitated as she approached the wall she'd have to scale. That pause killed her momentum, and she didn't even come close to succeeding.

She didn't give up, though. As he watched, she swung around and took another run at the wall. She failed the second attempt, too, and the third, and the fourth. She had heart, he'd give her that much. What she didn't have was a training partner. The wall was at maximum height. There was no way she'd be able to get over it without someone to give her a boost.

She crouched down to retie her shoes, and he jogged over, one hand up to shield his face from the stinging sleet. "Training partner wussed out because of the weather, huh?"

"I don't have a training partner. I need to figure out a

way to do this—." She looked up, and her lovely face went wide-eyed with shock. "Holy hell, you're Sergei Molotov!"

Bast be praised, she was a fan. "I am. Nice to meet you, instructor...?"

She blushed. "Me? Oh, no. I don't teach here. I'm Tabitha Willows, I work in the library. I'm just out, uh..." she gave the wall a vague wave of her hand.

"Testing your limits, Ms. Willows?" He asked.

"Yes, exactly. And please call me Tabi. Everyone does. I have to confess, I'm a bit of a fan. I was in your lecture last week about edible plants of the tundra. Oh, and your talk on cold weather survival tactics, and um... the one about basic shelter design."

How the hell had he missed this little beauty if she'd been to all his lectures? Some hunter he was. He held out his hand. "It's a pleasure, Tabi. Call me Sergei. And what do you mean, you don't have a partner?"

Her blush deepened. "Well, all the instructors work out with each other, and the cadets have regular training, of course. I just wanted to see if I could do it."

She glowered at the wall. "And I can, apart from this stupid thing."

"That's because you're not thinking outside the box." It was one of his trademark phrases.

"Oh!" She straightened a little and gifted him with a dazzling smile. "You're right!"

His ego and his cock both doubled in size in a matter of seconds. *Icy streams. Frozen lakes. Sleeping in snowbanks...* He ran through every cold memory he could recall until he got his errant ego and self-activating body parts under control.

4

"What do you need to get to the top of that wall?" he asked when he could think again.

"To grow six or seven inches?" she replied.

He had to discard the first three suggestions that popped into his mind when she mentioned seven inches. He'd clearly gone too long without getting laid. He cleared his throat. "I think you're the perfect height just the way you are, so how about another idea?"

She cocked her head in thought, exposing the side of her throat. Immediately, his brain was filled with visions of nibbling on her neck, her ear, and... *Whoa.* He went through his entire repertoire of cold memories again, this time accompanied by music from the movie, *Frozen. Let it go...*

By the time he was done, Tabi had jogged off to one side of the course and vaulted the chain-link fence that bordered the training area. Beyond it was an expanse of relatively pristine forest the shifters used to stretch their legs in their other forms, safely hidden from human eyes.

"Planning on shifting and tackling the wall that way?" he asked. Not that he thought she would. FUC encouraged staff and cadets alike to use discretion and only shift when it was essential. If the good people of this town knew what the academy was really for, they'd be at the gates with pitchforks and torches faster than you could say catnip cocktails.

Of course, that was one of the main reasons FUC existed: to keep the humans clueless about their not-so-human neighbours. Everyone in the area thought this was a training ground for animal rescuers. It was a fantastic cover, though he was still stunned they'd managed to get city hall to sign off on calling it the Animal Rescue Special House of Learning. That meant that the lettering over the gate proudly declared this place to be ARSHOL. There *had* to be bribes involved.

"Shifting? Here? Manes and tails, no. I need to do this without cheating. So, I'm doing what you said and looking outside the box. Aha! Got it." She pounced onto something hidden in the undergrowth with all the grace of a tiger cub attacking its own tail. One minute she was there and the next she was gone, though he could hear her well enough. "Ack! Mud!" There was a pause and then a yelp. "And thorns!"

He bit back a chuckle and went over to help. "You alright?"

She was sprawled on the ground, half-covered in dirt, muck, and dead leaves, but she had a rueful smile on her face as she looked up at him. "Me? I'm just peachy. What girl doesn't want a free mud bath?"

"I thought the point of those was to put it on your skin, not your clothes?" He crouched at her side and started working on detangling her from the patch of blackberry vines she'd fallen into. This close, he noticed her hair was dyed several shades of deep blue and purple. He wouldn't have pegged her as the type, but maybe the sweet little librarian had a wild streak. He caught her scent, too, and what he registered confused him. She almost smelled like an equine shifter, but everything he sensed told him she was a predator, not prey. What *was* she?

"I've got it on my skin, too. And in places not discussed in polite company."

Fuck. At this rate, he'd be humming the entire sound-track of that blasted movie on a loop to keep his mind out of the gutter. "Believe me when I tell you that I am not even close to polite company."

She freed her legs from the last of the brambles and laughed. "I know. I've seen your show, remember? There are entire sections that are nothing but bleeps. You must have given the censors conniptions."

"One of the many reasons the show isn't live." He got to his feet and offered her a hand up.

"The other being, you couldn't risk having to shift on camera?" Her fingers closed around his, and a flash of heat passed between them. He had to resist the urge to tug her into his arms.

"That's a big reason, yeah. It hasn't happened often, but if it does, we destroy everything, then and there. Memory cards, recording equipment, all of it."

"I wondered. I didn't even realize you were a shifter until they announced you were going to lecture here." Tabi started to brush herself off, then stopped with a disconsolate sigh. "I'm a mess."

"You are. But since I just spent the better part of a week in the bush myself, I figure this means we match." He'd managed a brutally cold but necessary dip in a partially frozen river this morning before they broke camp and encouraged everyone else to do the same. The thought of a bus full of unwashed shifter funk had been enough to get most of them into the water for at least a few seconds.

She turned her attention to the mountains that rose

into the sky. "I haven't made it up there yet. I bet it's beautiful."

"It is. It's also still winter. Snow on the ground, ice in the rivers. Ask the agents I just brought back how cold it was."

"Cold doesn't bother me," she shrugged.

"Then why haven't you gone hiking?"

She sighed. "That's a long story."

"Then you can tell it to me over dinner." He didn't wait for her to answer. He hefted the log she'd been struggling with out of the muck, slung it over his shoulder, and started back to the obstacle course. "I like your solution to the wall, by the way. This should do the trick nicely."

"Thanks." She passed him at a graceful lope and vaulted the fence with ease.

He was tempted to drop his burden and chase after her. He really did love the chase, especially when the prey was pretty enough to eat. She stopped on the other side of the fence and turned for him to catch up so she could help him with the log. She carried it the rest of the way herself, a silent reminder she wanted to do this on her own.

He stood back as she set up her makeshift platform, aware she hadn't agreed to dinner with him, yet. He wasn't going anywhere until she'd said yes. He was a patient hunter, and this was one morsel he didn't plan on letting slip away.

2

Manes and fucking tails, she was actually *talking* to Sergei Molotov. The man was sex on a stick. All whipcord muscle and white-blonde hair. He had a week's worth of pale beard on his chiselled jaw, which only added to his sex appeal. Not to mention that soft Russian accent of his sent her brain in all sorts of indecent directions. She'd gone to every one of his lectures over the last few weeks, staying in the back, out of the way, not even claiming a seat for fear someone with more right to be there would tell her to leave. And now, she was having a conversation with him. More than that, he'd asked her to dinner. She was sure she didn't need a boost to get over that wall right now. She was floating three feet off the fucking ground.

He didn't say a word as she positioned the log and then tested it for stability. She was not going to fall on her ass in front of him if she could help it. Well, not again. If she wiped out on the wall this time, he'd probably write her off as hopeless and leave before she said yes to his dinner invitation.

Crap. She hadn't said yes yet! Had she hit her head when she'd fallen? That had to be it. Wait! If she had a concussion, had she imagined the whole thing? Maybe she was still out cold in the woods.

Her inner beast gave a vague snort of annoyance. Okay, she wasn't hallucinating. Good. Then she better answer him before he took her silence to mean she wasn't interested. She was oh so very interested. She turned to face Sergei, who somehow managed to look sexy as hell despite the wild-man-of-the-woods look he had going on.

"Dinner sounds great. We can trade stories, though I'm pretty sure I only have one of interest. I'm just a librarian. I spend my time reading about other peoples' adventures. You've been living yours for years."

"But I know all my own stories. All I know about you is your name. I look forward to correcting that tonight." He nodded to the wall. "After you show this wall what you're made of."

Just the way he spoke sent a delicious tingle down her spine. She wasn't sure why someone with his looks and fame wanted to spend time with a nobody like her, but she already knew she'd remember the night she had dinner with Sergei Molotov until the day she died.

She flashed him a smile she hoped was cute and confident and raised her fist in salute. "Wall versus Tabi, the rematch."

"Kick its tail," he called to her as she jogged away, taking a quick lap to limber up again before facing her adversary.

It wasn't easy to focus on the wall when all she wanted to do was look at Sergei. He was watching her, too, tracking her every move like a predator stalking his next meal. Goosebumps chased over the back of her neck. Survival instincts be damned, she'd happily let herself get eaten by him any day.

Pay attention, or the only thing anyone will be eating is crow!

She adjusted her stride, locked her eyes on the wall, and went for it. Her foot landed squarely on the log, giving her the added reach she needed to grasp the top. She managed to walk herself up the vertical surface sideways, and when she got a leg over the top, she whooped in triumph. From there, it only took her a few seconds to haul herself up and hop down the far side. Thanks to research, Sergei's advice, and YouTube videos, she could now tackle any obstacle on the course.

Her moment of euphoria was cut short when she hit a patch of mud and fell on her ass. Again. Frustrated, she slammed her hand into the sleet-soaked ground and bit back a snarl of frustration. Her vision turned red at the edges and she rushed to calm herself before her temper triggered a shift. The last thing she wanted was for Sergei to come around the wall and find himself face to face with an emotionally unstable unicorn. She wanted one dinner with him before he found out her secret and took the next off-ramp out of her life.

The red tint to her vision faded by the time the hot tiger shifter came into view.

"You and gravity are not the best of friends, huh? You okay?"

"Nothing hurt but my pride." She looked up at the wall. "I did it, though!"

"Yes, you did. Well done." He held out his hand, and she took it, happy for another excuse to touch him. His grip was firm, and his hands were warm despite the fact it was cold enough the sleet was changing to snow. Spring arrived a lot later to the Rockies than the coast where she'd grown up.

"Thank you for reminding me to look for another solution. I'm buying the drinks tonight. I think we've both earned it."

His brows rose in surprise. "The academy has a liquor license? No one told me this place had a bar."

"No bar. But I've got a bottle of Baileys in my room. I was going to suggest we doctor our coffees. I know I could use something hot and sweet right about now."

"You live here? I thought most of the non-teaching staff lived off-campus."

"They do." She flicked a lock of muddy hair out of her eyes. "It's all part of my strange tale. But for now, all you need to know is that I have Baileys. You in?"

"All in," he replied, and something in his voice made her breath catch in her throat. The part of her that remembered being prey screamed at her to run, but the rest of her turned into a quivering puddle of goo.

He took her hand and squeezed it. "Race you back to the main building?"

"You're on." She grinned, noting he hadn't called the place by it's official name. The WANC, or Working and Administration Networking Core, was one aconym most campus visitors stumbled over at first.

"Go!" He released her and took off at a dead run. She chased after him, lengthening her strides until they were running side by side. The snow stung her cheeks and the icy air was almost painful to breathe, but she loved it. Exercise was one of the few things that kept her calm and centred. When she was running, she forgot about her problems. It was the only time she and her new form were entirely in synch.

They raced pell-mell to the front doors of the main building. Every time one of them increased speed, the other managed to match it, but in the end, Sergei claimed victory by a couple of steps. They stopped to catch their breath in the entranceway, keeping to one side so they didn't block the flow of people coming and going.

"Not many people can outrun me in a sprint. I'm impressed," Tabi said.

Sergei shook some of the water and sleet from his hair. "My cardio training includes outrunning things that think I'm on the menu."

"But you're an apex predator!" Sergei was a Siberian tiger. In his animal form he could take out almost any land animal on the planet.

"I am. I also can't shift when I'm being filmed, or when we've got humans on the set. Doesn't happen often, but it means I need to be ready to deal with trouble without reverting to tooth and claw."

"I hear the instructors harp on that all the time. Shifting can't be our default response to danger." She shook her head. "My parents had another approach. They bought a huge farm on an island, far away from humans. It was basically one big shifter commune. Growing up, I was free to shift whenever I wanted. They wanted me to feel safe, so they didn't tell me about the dangers of the outside world until I was almost an adult."

"That had to be a shock for you."

"It was." She gestured around them. "When I applied for a job here, it was my parents' turn to be surprised. They still don't understand why I'd ever want to leave home."

"Then they don't know you very well. We've spoken for less than twenty minutes, and I can already tell you're not the kind to stay home and live a safe, quiet life."

"I'm a librarian. That's a pretty safe, quiet career choice," she pointed out.

"At a school that trains secret agents." He ran a hand through his hair, smoothing the sodden strands back from his face.

"Okay, you've got a point there." Without thinking, she reached out to wipe a trickle of water away before it dripped into his eyes. She left a smudge of mud on his brow, and she pulled her hand away in dismay. "Oops. I think I'm making it worse. Sorry."

He caught her hand and held it gently in his. "I'm good with a little mud. In fact, I quite like getting dirty if there's a pretty girl involved."

She blushed so hard her cheeks felt like they'd been dipped in kerosene and set on fire. Thankfully, he released her and stepped away before she babbled something so stupid she died of terminal embarrassment.

He wasn't done making her blush, though. "Where in this vast complex is your room? Please tell me it's close to the guest rooms, so I can be a proper gentleman and see you to your door?"

"I'm in the general area, yes." She was precisely six doors down from where he'd been assigned. She'd seen him walking down the hall not long after he arrived and peeked to see where he was staying. At the time, she thought that would be the closest she'd get.

"Then I shall escort you there." He offered her his arm in a gallant gesture that was totally out of place given their generally dishevelled state, but she took it with all the aplomb of a highborn lady of yesteryear. Albeit, a drenched and muddy one.

"Thank you, Lord Tiger."

He chuckled. "My full title should be Lord Sergei, Tiger of Siberia, chaser of all things fluffy, and king of all he surveys."

"In that case, you may call me Lady Tabitha, Defeater of walls, and disciple of thinking outside the box."

He shot her a sidelong glance. "Still no hints as to what your other form is, huh?"

"Nope. No hints. We're going to need liquor for that conversation."

"We are?"

"Definitely."

His voice dropped to a low, sultry rumble. "Hasn't anyone warned you that it's dangerous to tease a cat?"

"I thought you were supposed to avoid being too curious? Isn't that a fatal condition for felines?" She couldn't believe the words coming out of her mouth. She didn't flirt. Not well, anyway. Had she been possessed by a flirtatious demon?

He stopped and turned to face her. "Curiosity killed the cat." He leaned until his mouth was beside her ear and dropped his voice to a whisper. "But satisfaction brings us back, every time."

She uttered a sound somewhere between a gasp and a squeak. Not exactly sexy, but Sergei didn't seem to care. He moved away, winked, and continued walking as if nothing had happened.

He's just flirting. Guys do that. She reminded herself, but another voice was whispering from the back of her mind. *And cats like to play with their food. Maybe we're dessert.* Manes and tails, she hoped so, but the odds were not in her favour. The *incident* hadn't just changed who and what she was, it had killed her love-life deader than the dodo.

3

Sergei had been delighted to discover that Tabi's place was only a few steps down the hall from him. Despite being on campus for weeks, he'd somehow missed her until now. Was he really that rusty when it came to noticing women? Maybe his mother was right... not that he would ever admit that. One word and she'd decide to *help*. He'd be hip deep in eligible women before breakfast the next day. Worse, they'd be his mother's idea of suitable mate material. He loved his mother, but there wasn't any room in his life for the kind of mate she thought he needed. A quiet homemaker whose idea of adventure was hosting a dinner party for more than three other people.

It was too bad he hadn't met Tabi earlier. She was the first interesting woman he'd met in...he didn't do the math. Too depressing. Unfortunately, he was leaving the day after tomorrow, which meant he wouldn't have much time to enjoy her company.

"Bast giveth with one paw and taketh away with the other," he muttered to himself as he towelled his hair. His schedule didn't allow for much of a social life, something his mother brought up with alarming regularity.

He stretched again, doing a quick inventory of his aches and pains, and grudgingly admitted his mother had a point. At thirty-three, he was still in his prime, but sleeping rough for days on end and foraging for meals wasn't as fun as it used to be... and neither was waking up alone. With that thought in the forefront of his mind, he set his phone to vibrate and went to find his date for the evening.

He knocked on Tabi's door and was pleased when it opened barely a second later.

She looked stunning. Her long hair hung in waves over her shoulders, and now it was dry he could clearly see the deep blue and purple streaks that ran through her dark tresses. She'd worn a simple black sweater dress that came to mid-thigh, and leggings that...he grinned. Her leggings had tigers printed on them.

"Hello, again. You look lovely." He deliberately let his gaze linger on her long legs. "Nice pants."

Her brown eyes danced with merriment, but she managed not to crack a smile. "Thank you. I thought you'd appreciate them."

Hell yes, he appreciated them. In fact, he was a little jealous of the tiny tigers. They were a lot closer to her than he was. "Very much." He offered her his arm again. "Shall we?"

"Yes please. I confess I'm starving. I hope the ravenous hordes haven't picked the place clean before we get there." She took his arm, and he breathed in her scent. Soap and cosmetics, and underneath it, that same mysterious something he couldn't identify. What was she?

"Have no fear, I've made arrangements. We'll be well fed tonight."

"Arrangements?"

"Mhmm."

"No details?"

"Nope. Not unless you want to tell me what kind of shifter you are?"

"Sneaky, but no." She patted her small purse. "Drinks first."

"Brave woman, keeping a tiger in suspense."

"I'm not that brave. I just..." her smile faded, and she turned her face away. "It's all very new to me, and I'm not good at talking about it, yet."

Whoa. How could her shifter side be new? Shifters were born, not created. Unless... "Involuntary experimentation?" There were more than a few mad scientist types out there, some living, some as dead as disco. The Master-mind and the Bunyip Instistute were two he'd heard about, but he knew there had to be others.

Tabi nodded but stayed silent. They were walking by a group of cadets and clearly, she didn't feel like talking about it around other people. He was so distracted by Tabi's distress he almost missed the way the cadets reacted to them. He was used to being noticed, it came with the territory, but none of them were looking at him. They were watching Tabi warily, and they all shuffled a little closer to the walls as she walked by. *Odd.*

He caught a few snippets of hushed conversation.

"That's Stabitha."

"Freak."

"Psycho."

Tabi hunched her shoulders and kept her eyes on the floor in front of them. Sergei wanted to smack the bunch of them into the middle of next week. He settled for growling in warning while fixing them with a stare that had been known to send wild grizzlies hightailing it into the trees.

Once they were alone again, he reached over to cover her hand where it rested on his arm. "That happen a lot?"

"All the time."

"Have you spoken to Director Cooper about it?" If she hadn't he would. Those cadets were training to protect all shifters. What kind of agents would they be if they were biased against the ones they were supposed to be helping?

"You mean report them? No. I wouldn't do that. It's just words, right? Words can't hurt me."

He knew that wasn't true, but he didn't argue with her. He'd have a word with Director Alyce Cooper before he left and let her know there was a problem. Odds were good she already knew, but it couldn't hurt to point it out. "Forget about them. They're not on tonight's agenda."

"Want to tell me what is? I still don't even know where we're going."

"To a private dining room across from the cafeteria. It's just you, me, a three-course meal, and your illicit stash of Bailey's."

"Just the two of us?" Her relief was so evident it was all he could do not to stop right there and hug her.

"No one else. Unless you'd like a chaperone?" He

raised a hand. "I swear I'll be a gentleman, at least until dessert."

That garnered a small smile. "Only until dessert, huh?"

"I get a little wild once chocolate is involved."

"Me, too. And yes, I'm fine without a chaperone. In fact, it will make it easier to tell you the story. I don't talk about it much."

They made it to the small dining room he'd requested without further incident. He walked her to her chair, pulling it out for her and everything. The room was small and only modestly furnished. A few round tables, chairs to seat maybe a dozen people, and not much else. Their table had a simple black table cloth on it, with the same standard dishes and silverware they used to feed the masses next door. Dinner had been delivered, too, and sat on a room service style cart next to the table.

"I didn't know this room even existed. I usually eat in the main hall or take a tray back to my room. Then again, I'm staff. I don't think the kitchen would be thrilled if I asked for VIP treatment like this."

"There are some perks to my job that I admit I enjoy more than I should." He pulled a couple of emergency candles out of his back pocket, lit them, and then held the ends over his lighter long enough to soften the wax before sticking three of them together on a plate. "Tada, mood lighting."

"Very nice. You should offer to teach a special MacGyver 101 class for dating."

He shook his head. "Duct tape and dating preparation are two things that should never be uttered in the same sentence. Besides, the cadets are supposed to be here to learn, not chase tail."

"You think so? From what I've seen, they're pretty good at multitasking." She pulled a small bottle of Baileys Irish Cream out of her purse and set it on the table. "As promised."

Tabi paused to pour a generous portion of liqueur into two mugs and then filled them to the brim with coffee, adding a dollop of fresh whipped cream from the cart.

He raised his mug in salute. "What shall we drink to?"

"New friends?" she suggested.

He considered that for all of a nanosecond before rejecting it. Too limiting. You didn't get naked and wild with friends, and by Bast's fluffy tail, that's exactly what he wanted to do with Tabi. "To new beginnings."

"I like it. New beginnings." She touched her mug to his, then took a sip. "Oh, that's good."

He would have agreed with her, but his ability to form words keeled over and died as she swiped her tongue across her lips to catch a stray bit of cream. Neurons misfired in his brain, all the blood in his body flowed south, and he forgot to breathe for a few seconds.

She looked at him and frowned in concern. "Is yours alright? Did I add too much Baileys?"

He managed to suck in a quick breath before he turned purple. "Great. Just great." He took another sip, then set the mug down and got to his feet. Fuck subtle.

He walked around the table to her, leaned down and met her gaze. "I need to kiss you right now."

"You do?"

He cupped her cheek in his hand. Her skin was soft

and heated beneath his fingers. The desire to pull her in close and kiss her until she was breathless was almost more than he could take. First, he'd kiss her, then he wanted to get her naked and whisper dirty things in her ear so he could watch her blush all over. "More than anything. May I?"

Her eyes darkened with desire and her lips parted as she breathed her next words. "Yes, please."

That's all he needed. His lips brushed hers and his senses exploded. She was soft, warm, and tasted of whipped cream and peppermint toothpaste. He drank her in, and the more he experienced, the more he wanted her. He speared his fingers into her hair, drawing her head back so he could take their kiss deeper. He nipped at her lower lip and she parted her mouth with a soft moan that rolled through him like the first warning rumbles of an avalanche. He plumbed the depths of her mouth as her hands roamed over his chest and shoulders, soft touches that made him wish they were already naked so he could feel her fingers on his flesh.

His phone buzzed, but he ignored it. Whoever was calling him could leave a damned message.

He took her hands and held them, coaxing her to stand. The moment she rose from her chair he wrapped his arms around her and pulled her in close. *Better.*

Her fingers stroked through his hair and down the back of his neck. The sensation made him quiver and sent another jolt of lust straight to his cock. The things he wanted to do to this woman…

"Sergei…" she whispered his name against his lips.

"Do you want to stop?" He hoped like hell the answer

was no, but he had to be sure. This hadn't been what he'd intended when he'd invited her for dinner, but now he'd had a taste…

"Stop? No. Definitely not. But maybe…" He felt the heat of her blush. "Does the door lock?"

And once again, she'd rendered him speechless. All higher functions ceased operations and he swore his common sense had left a sign on the door that read "Out to lunch. Come back later."

He tried to get his brain to work. Checking the door meant letting go of her. Definitely a negative. But if the door locked? That was a positive.

He kissed her again while struggling toward some kind of decision, but before he could commit to a course of action, the universe made the call for him. Someone rapped on the door to their room, proving once and for all that the universe had a lousy sense of timing.

4

If it got any hotter in here Tabi suspected they'd set off the smoke alarms. Her fantasies about what it would be like to kiss Sergei couldn't hold a candle to the real thing. All her plans to be honest and upfront with him before anything happen went up in flames the second he asked if he could kiss her. At that point, a snowball in hell had better survival odds than her good intentions. The knock at the door had probably saved her from throwing the last tattered remnants of her caution to the four winds.

The door opened before either of them could move.

"Sergei? Sorry to interrupt your dinner. I've got some news you need to hear." Alyce Cooper walked into the room, took one look at the two of them, and stopped dead in her tracks. It was the first time Tabi had seen the normally unflappable academy director speechless.

"Sorry. No one in the kitchen mentioned you had company tonight." Alyce nodded to Tabi. "Ms. Willows."

"Director Cooper." Tabi untangled herself from Sergei and stepped back, half hoping the earth had cracked open and she could vanish forever beneath the surface. Death by magma was preferable to staying here under her boss's unblinking gaze.

Sergei turned to face Alyce, positioning himself so that Tabi was shielded behind him. "Director. What's so important you had to interrupt my first decent meal in days?"

Tabi held her breath. No one talked to the director that way. She was a no-nonsense sort who would happily chew up and spit out anyone who didn't toe the line. And since Alyce was a llama shifter, spitting was one of her specialties.

Alyce didn't so much as bat one of her overly long lashes at Sergei's tone. "Play nice, Sergei, or I'll tell Tabi about that mission to Moose Jaw."

"You wouldn't. We vowed to take that one to our graves."

Alyce just stood there.

"Fine. Fine. I'll be nice. Welcome, Director. Lovely evening. Delighted to see you."

Alyce snorted. "And I thought you were in show business. You didn't even try to sell that."

"No motivation." He deadpanned. "But honestly, Alyce, why are you here? It's got to be important for you to deliver the news yourself."

She pulled out a piece of paper and handed it to him. "You've been MUFF DIVEd."

Sergei stiffened. "What? No! It was just a kiss."

Tabi stepped around him to get a look at the paper and caught Alyce hiding a laugh behind her hand. Since the director seemed incapable of speech, she explained.

"MUFF is short for Merrily United Furry Friends against the unethical treatment of non-sentient animals by shifters."

He shot her a confused look. "Seems like the acronym is missing a few letters."

"Don't look at me, I'm just a librarian. I didn't name them."

Alyce got herself together and finished the explanation. "The second part stands for Disclosure of Intent against Vile Enemies. It's basically MUFF's version of a declaration of war."

"Who are these people again?" Sergei asked.

"MUFF is a problem group that appeared after you left us. They started out as a minor disruptive force, but they're popping up more often these days." Alyce pointed to the paper. "Basically, they're targeting you because you eat animals on your show."

"A bunch of wackadoodle shifters are up in arms because I eat meat? I'm a tiger. What am I supposed to eat, tofu?"

Alyce shrugged. "It's more because you hunt and kill your own meat and teach others how to do it. The animals you kill haven't been certified as non-shifters, and well..." She sighed and tapped the paper. "It's all in there. The important part is that you're on their radar, and they've staked out your show's next shooting location. They're not very stable, or smart, but they are disruptive. You're going to need to postpone the shoot."

Tabi expected Sergei to swear, or argue, but he just hummed and kept reading, his face impassive. When he finished, he nodded. "I'll make a few calls. I'm not putting my people at risk over this. You good with me staying here a few extra days?"

"You're welcome to stay as long as you like. In fact..." Alyce cleared her throat. "I was wondering if, given this news, you'd reconsider taking some of our best cadets out on a training excursion. A short one."

"You are a very sneaky woman."

"Of course I am, I'm FUC."

Tabi tried to move away so the two could make their plans in peace, but Sergei caught her hand and drew her back to his side. "No more than six students, and I'll want another staff member along, too."

"I can recommend several instructors who would be—"

Sergei cut Alyce off with a wave of his hand. "I'll take Tabi."

Tabi felt like a bug under glass the way Alyce was staring at her. "You want to take Ms. Willows with you. A librarian? Do *you* want to go on this trip, Ms. Willows?" The question was loaded with undertones. Alyce knew Tabi's situation, and how tenuous her control over her new form was. She was giving her a chance to bow out.

Tabi thought about it for all of three milliseconds. Sergei's lack of communication skills aside, it was a once in a lifetime opportunity. If ever she was going to try to step outside her comfort zone again, this was the moment. "I'd really like to go, Director Cooper. If you're agreeable?"

Alyce blinked. "You want to go? The cadets..."

"Will be too busy trying to stay alive to have time for anything else." At least, Tabi hoped so. She could handle their sly looks and whispered comments, but she wasn't sure Sergei would be as tolerant. And she still hadn't told him what she was. She'd have to do that tonight, so he had time to change his mind.

Sergei grunted. "Damn right they will. Some of them need a boot to the ass, Director. There's no place in FUC for judgement or bias, and I saw both tonight."

He wrapped his arm around her shoulders protectively, and Tabi leaned in a little more than was appropriate, but dammit, the man was hot when he was growly and protective, especially when the one he was protecting was her.

"That's part of what they're here to learn. I'll send you the information you'll need. Names, shifter types, backgrounds. You'll want them prepared with the same kits as the agents, I assume?"

"Please. And remind them no outside food or extra equipment."

"I'll make the arrangements. And I really do appreciate this, Sergei. I know the cadets will, too."

He snorted. "Ask them how they feel after we get back. They might have a different opinion by then. Oh, and can you please make sure all the cadets are hardy types? No fluffy prey species or delicate birds this time around."

"No fluff. Got it. When can you be ready?"

He cocked his head in thought. "As much as it pains me to say it, the sooner we go, the better. The colder weather won't last much longer, and I'd rather not be up there when all that snow starts to melt. Mud. Flooding. Treacherous footing in any streams we need to ford—it's a lot of extra risks."

Alyce nodded. "Agreed."

He sighed. "Can they be ready to go by tomorrow?"

The director looked insulted. "We're training agents here, not delicate flowers. Of course they'll be ready."

"I'll send you our planned route and coordinates later, along with a pickup location for day three."

Tabi finally found the nerve to interrupt the two as they made plans. "Uh, what can I do to help? That's why you want me along, isn't it?"

"Director Cooper, you are going to want assessments on the cadets' progress, yes?"

The director nodded. "I know that's not your usual thing, but yes, I would."

"And I am not good with paperwork. One of the many reasons I'm no longer an agent. Tabi will help me assess the students."

She brightened. Organizing and recording information was something she did well.

"You're sure?" Alyce pressed.

"I'm sure." The experts kept telling her she needed to push her boundaries and try to find a new normal, one that included eating meat and transforming into something that looked like an oversized My Little Pony after a goth makeover.

"She is sure. I am sure. We will do this." Sergei's accent was getting thicker by the second. "You go now. I'm starving, and apparently, I'm only going to have a few meals to carb-load before I'm back to foraging for food."

The director smirked a little. "I'm going, I'm going. Predators. Always so pushy."

"Prey shifters, always trying to stay in groups." Sergei waved Alyce toward the door. "Shoo."

Once they were alone again, Tabi turned to Sergei. "I can't believe you just told the director to *shoo*."

"She interrupted my dinner. And my dessert." He bent over to brush a gentle kiss to the top of Tabi's head, making it very clear just what *dessert* he was referring to. "I'm sorry about that. I had no idea anyone would interrupt us."

"It's okay. Thanks to the director, we're going to have more time together." She took a deep breath. "That is, if you still want me along once I tell you what I am."

He jerked a thumb at his broad chest. "I know you are a predator, like me."

She slipped out of his grasp and dropped into her chair. The second her ass hit the seat, she added another dollop of Bailey's to her mug and started drinking. It took four swallows before she felt ready to answer him. "I am now, yes. Sort of."

"Sort of?"

"They don't actually know how to classify me."

He'd taken a seat while she downed her Irish coffee and looked at her intently. "Why not?"

"Because whatever they did to me made me into something new."

"What are you?"

"Equus Fantasia Gothicus," she replied.

His brows hit his hairline. "And what the fuck is that, exactly?"

"I'm a unicorn, Sergei. The only one in existence."

He didn't laugh or let go of her hand, but his brow

furrowed into creases deep enough to get a geologist excited. "Unicorns aren't predators."

"How do you know?" She pointed to her forehead. "Know any other horny horses? Um, I mean horned, not horny. I mean I am, but I'm not... and... Gods, I'm babbling now, aren't I?"

His eyes danced with mirth but he managed to keep a straight face. "Not at all. So you are Equus Fantasia... what was that last bit?"

"Gothicus. It's just nerd speak for a black, goth-looking unicorn." She tugged on a lock of her hair. "This isn't a dye job. It changed the first time I shifted and stayed this way."

"Black unicorn. Okay. But why don't you talk about it?"

"Because most people freak a bit when they find out. Especially since me and my shifter side aren't exactly in synch. She's kind of temperamental." *And stabby.*

"That's understandable. How long ago did this happen? *What* happened?"

"A few months ago I got a fancy invitation to an all-exclusive shifter resort that was opening up. I'd been looking at all sorts of vacation packages, and I figured I'd entered a contest and didn't realize it. I thought it was my lucky day. Boy, was I wrong."

"The whole thing was a trap?"

"It was. They drugged us a few at a time so no one noticed. I got one day on the beach before I ate the wrong breakfast pastry and woke up in a cage. I bet the doughnut wasn't even vegan. I knew it tasted too good to be true."

"Who did this to you?"

"I don't know. FUC handled it and said it was 'need to know' information."

"They didn't tell you who was behind it?" His tone had a hint of a growl to it, now.

"Knowing wouldn't change anything. What's done is done. I've been poked and prodded and tested by every expert FUC has. The change is permanent. I just have to deal with it."

"Did they hurt you?" It was a question not many had asked, and none of them had said it with a murderous gleam in their eyes. Like he'd happily kill the ones to blame if she said yes.

It was a new experience. Her parents were pacifists. A pair of gentle vegans who hadn't known what to do for their daughter, or how to deal with the changes she'd undergone. The Academy staff had welcomed her back and given her much-needed support, but no one had made her feel the way Sergei did. He wasn't afraid of her. There was no pity in his eyes. He hadn't run from the room. In fact, he hadn't let go of her hand.

She told him the truth. More of it than she'd told anyone but the agent who took her statement. Not even her parents knew everything. She hadn't known how to tell them. "They hurt me. I was pretty banged up by the time the rescue came. They believe some of it was from my attempts to tear the cage apart, but... not all of it. I was sedated a lot of the time, but I remember bits and pieces." She shivered and pushed the dark memories away. If they took hold, her other half would come out.

"You okay? We don't have to talk about this."

"We do. You need to know before you decide if you really want me along on this trip. I'm not stable, Sergei. And my other half can be dangerous. The injuries I suffered were retaliation for killing the two men who were inside my cage the first time I woke up. They never had a chance." And that was the real horror of what they'd done to her. They'd stolen her sense of self and made her into a killer.

She'd thought he'd recoil from her, or at least reconsider. The last thing she expected him to do was to throw back his head and laugh.

"It's not a laughing matter."

"That depends on what side of the table you're sitting on. You are afraid of your new nature. Yet, here you sit, having dinner with someone who was born a predator. I'm laughing because I know I'm far more dangerous than you are."

She scowled at him. "Want to bet? The cadets call me Stabitha. All that whispering in the hallway? That's because I lost control one day and stabbed a hole in the old card catalogue. Paper flew everywhere, the wood shattered, it was a mess!"

He raised a brow. "Messy, yes. But hardly dangerous. Except to antiquated filing systems."

"We keep it around as part of the cadets' training. They have to learn not to rely on computers for everything."

"A good lesson. And I think that's what you need, too."

"A lesson in what?"

"How to be a predator." He gave her a smile that melted an alarming number of her brain cells. "When I am

34

done with you, you will not be afraid of what you are, Tabi Willows. But other people should be."

The part of her that used to be a thoroughbred horse shied away from the idea, but that wasn't who she was anymore. Meditation, yoga, and self-affirmations weren't working, so it was time to try something else. Either that, or she would wind up running laps around the obstacle course every day for the rest of her life. No one needed that much cardio. "Alright, Sergei Molotov. Teach me."

His grin turned utterly wicked. "With pleasure."

5

One kiss from Tabi wasn't enough. Unfortunately, he hadn't considered that need when he'd arranged for the next outing to start less than twenty-four hours later. He should have asked for a few days off, first. Bad planning on his part. Instead of a leisurely dinner and conversation that might have led to an unforgettable night in bed, they'd spent the rest of their time coming up with a plan for their last-minute adventure.

She'd made notes on her phone, and when he'd woken up this morning, he discovered she'd sent him an itemized list, a timeline for their departure, packing lists, names and pertinent details for every cadet on the trip, and several pages of indexed notes and photos of what flora and fauna they might come across in their trek, and which ones were edible. All he had to do was arrange for copies to be made, and he'd have handouts for the cadets. The woman was amazing.

He looked over the list of names of the cadets on this trip. Four men and two women, all highly rated in both academics and physical training. Tabi had presented him with laminated copies of their information, with space for him to make notes and a collection of waterproof markers to go with them. It was something he hadn't even considered, but it would make assessing the cadets a lot easier.

The cadets were only one of his worries, though. MUFF was another one. He'd read through the files last night. They were robe-wearing wackos, and Alyce hadn't been kidding when she said they were tenacious. If that group of New Age ding-dongs got wind of where he was, they were just as likely to show up at the academy and cause trouble, which wouldn't be good for anyone.

While he was musing, the cadets wandered over to the bus, some of them solo, three of them arriving together. He recognized them right off as part of the group who'd been making comments about Tabi last night. *Son of a bitch.*

Once all six of them were present, he put two fingers to his lips and whistled. "Line up along the side of the bus. I need to do a quick inspection of your gear."

They formed up quickly, which was gratifying. Tabi had been inside the bus talking with Chet, the driver, but she reappeared, hovering on the steps, clearly uncertain. He gestured for her to step out, and then pointed to the ground beside him. He wanted to make it clear from the very start that she was with him.

"I'm Sergei Molotov. For those of you who don't know, this is Tabitha Willows. She's a member of the academy staff and will be part of the leadership team." He gestured to her, then himself. "Leadership." Then he pointed to them. "Cadets. Clear?"

They all nodded, though he noted that several of them eyed Tabi dubiously.

"Good. There's something you need to understand about this trip. I'm saying this now, because I don't want to hear any complaints later."

He waited until all eyes were on him. "You are not going to enjoy the next three days. You will be cold, wet, tired, and hungry. You will eat what you can forage and shelter under what you can build. You will listen to my instructions and follow them to the letter."

Several of them stirred uneasily. *Good.*

He walked to the line of backpacks arranged near the front of the bus and picked up one. "This contains the same basic supplies as an agent's kit, with one addition. Each bag has a single MRE in it. When you eat it is up to each of you, but I recommend waiting until at least the second night." He handed the bag to Tabi. "Give one of these to each of the cadets once I've had a look at their gear, please."

She nodded, and he thought he saw a glimmer of amusement in her lovely brown eyes. She liked it when he got bossy, huh? Then she was going to enjoy the next few days immensely. He took these training sessions seriously. There were too many things that could go wrong if anyone, even agents, were left without firm instructions.

He gave each cadet a quick once over, making sure they had clothing and gear sufficient for the trek. They'd followed instructions more or less, though he found a couple of contraband candy bars and a hipflask full of what smelled like cheap scotch. He confiscated it all, garnering muttered protests. Of course, it was the trio from last night that were trying to sneak extra food. They might be the best cadets on campus, but unfortunately for them, they were about to leave the grounds, which meant they were on *his* turf for the next few days.

He pocketed the flask and met the sulky gaze of its former owner, a python shifter named Joshua Keane. "That's mine," the dark-haired shifter muttered.

"It was." Sergei patted his pocket. "And now it's mine, along with your unquestioning obedience and respect. Clear?"

Joshua gave an almost imperceptible nod, but his dark eyes slid over to look at Tabi. "She's a *librarian*. Do I have to take her orders?"

"She's a member of the staff and part of my team. So yes, you have to listen to her."

Sergei held up his clipboard. "This is part of your training. You will be graded. And if you can't follow orders, then maybe you're not in the right place."

The next cadet in line whispered, "The other instructors don't talk to us like that."

He swung his attention to the one who'd spoken. "Name?"

"Me?" He was a twenty-something male with dark, slicked back hair, and sharp features. "Uh, Guy Harris."

"Well, Guy. Let me explain something to you. I am not an instructor. I'm not even FUC anymore. If you get on the bus you'll have to do things my way." He pointed to the bus' open door, then to the main building. "None of you have to come on this trip. You can head back inside right now."

None of them moved.

"Great. Now we've got that cleared up, take your packs and get on board. Departure in two minutes."

He and Tabi moved out of earshot, which was a significant distance when dealing with shifters. "How was that?"

"I think they're mildly traumatized. What are you going to do with the contraband?"

"Keep it with me. They can have the junk food on the ride back. The booze?" He patted his pocket. "Firestarter."

She hid a smile behind her hand. "You're wicked."

He wanted to kiss her so badly it was a physical ache, but he couldn't. Not here. "Sweetheart, you have no idea."

She blushed, right to the tips of her adorable ears. He had never been good with temptation, and right now, she was his personal bag of catnip, dangling just out of reach.

He cleared his throat. "You ready for this?"

The blush faded. "Honestly, I don't know. But I need to do it, anyway. It's only three days, right? What's the worst that could happen?"

6

The bus rolled out of sight, leaving them alone in the Parks Canada parking lot. Watching it go, Tabi had a sudden urge to chase after it. What was she doing out here? She hadn't been camping since her teens, and that had involved tents, sing-a-longs, and enough s'mores to satiate a ravening pack of dingoes. If dingoes ate s'mores. Did they? She'd have looked that up on the internet, but Sergei's rules included a total ban on electronics. That didn't bother her much. Her family's farm was so remote it hadn't even gotten broadband until she was in high school. She was used to being disconnected from the world. The cadets weren't, and they were already in withdrawal.

She took a breath and reminded herself that this wasn't much different from a normal day back home. She'd lived off the grid most of her life. She could do this. If Sergei had doubts, then he wouldn't have brought her along. Of course, that tiger was so sure of himself he'd probably never had a doubt in his whole life.

The cadets gathered together by the trailhead, hunched into their parkas, toques pulled down low over their ears as an icy wind blasted them with occasional flurries of blowing snow. Winter was still holding on at this elevation. They all had the gear to cope with the conditions, but by the time they got back home, the chilly spring weather down there would feel like a tropical vacation.

Sergei had continued his hard-nosed act for the entire drive, which meant she hadn't had anyone to talk to. She had hoped they could chat to pass the time, or maybe he would give her some idea how he intended to help her embrace her new nature. He'd napped instead. *Cats.*

The cadets talked among themselves, mostly complaining about not being allowed to take their phones so they had something to do on the drive. She got the sense that some of them were still in denial about how tough the next few days would be.

Tensions had cranked up when they stopped for gas. Everyone had debarked to stretch their legs for five minutes, but when the time passed, only half the cadets were back on the bus. The others had wandered off.

She'd tracked down Janice in the station's grotty washroom, while Sergei retrieved Joshua and Guy from inside the store. They were in the middle of buying coffees for everyone, so Sergei had let it slide with nothing more than a gruff warning to keep better track of the time.

She wasn't sure what to make of this part of his personality. It was a far cry from the man she'd watched on television or the suave charmer who'd offered to help a stranger and then kissed her senseless a few hours later.

She couldn't tell which of his personas were the real Sergei. Hell, maybe they all were. Not everyone was as boring as she was - at least before the *incident* had turned her into an unstable freak.

"Alright, people. Now the fun starts!" Sergei marched over to where the others were standing. "It's a nice, easy two-hour hike to our first objective. The faster we get there, the more daylight you'll have left to set up your shelters and see what you can find for food. Check the handouts in your kits and keep your eyes open as you walk, if you see something that might be edible call out and I'll take a look. This isn't just a walk in the woods, this is grocery shopping."

Annie, a bear shifter with a sunny smile not even the current weather could dampen, laughed out loud. "Any Kraft Dinner trees out here? Or maybe a patch of Easter Crème egg bushes?"

"You never know." Sergei actually cracked a smile, raised a hand in the hair, and made a circling gesture. "Move out!"

They set off a brisk pace, Sergei leading the way. The snow had collapsed enough to make the trail easy to follow, but the forest was still more white than green, and the drifts between the trees looked deep enough to swallow up anyone foolish enough to wander too far off the path. Bathroom breaks were going to be an adventure.

Soon all conversation stopped and all she could hear was the crunch of boots on snow and heavy breathing. If this was Sergei's idea of easy, she was grateful she'd started running lately or they'd be leaving her at the side of the trail to fend for herself before they made their first camp.

After twenty minutes or so, Sergei tapped Annie to take the lead. He watched the rest march past him, then fell into step beside Tabi. "You good?"

"Fine. All this exercise is keeping me toasty warm. You?"

"Regretting the fact we can't snuggle together for warmth tonight. Other than that, all's well."

"I imagine anyone with a furry side will wish they could shift forms once it's time to sleep."

Sergei had made it clear that shifting was only to be done in an emergency.

"For me, it's not the extra fur. It's the ability to curl into a ball and tuck my face under my tail. Very comfy."

She laughed. "I'll have to take your word on it. Horses aren't built for that. We just stand with our heads down-wind and endure."

"But you're not a horse anymore," he reminded her.

"Still shaped like one. Just a weaponized version."

"There's more to your change than just a horn and a temper. That's what you have to accept. You're different now."

She bristled, not because he was wrong, but because she wasn't used to being pushed about it. "How would you know? You only met me yesterday."

He ignored her outburst. "What species were your parents?"

"Dad's a horse, mom's a black-tailed deer."

"And you already told me you were raised in a commune, and you were eating vegan doughnuts. Which, by the way, is an abomination against pastries, but I digress. You were a prey animal. A soft little morsel for someone like me. You're not prey anymore, and that changes everything."

She choked and felt an alarming surge of outrage. "Morsel? Is that how you see shifters like me?"

"Well, yes." He pointed to the cadets ahead of him. "This group is at the top of their class. They're also predators. Bear, coyote, python, lynx, and an otter."

"Otters are hardly apex predators," she sniffed. "They're fuzzy little bundles of cute, and Danny isn't a predator. He's a moose."

"River otters might be cute, but sea otters are a hundred pounds of nasty who drown dogs for fun. As for Danny? If you got him riled, he'd take down every other species here, except for maybe me and the bear."

"You're speciest!" She would never have expected someone like him to hold such outdated ideas. It was the twenty-first century! Any shifter, no matter what their species, could do anything they set their mind to.

"I'm a realist."

"You're… something." She wanted to walk away from him, but that seemed a bit pointless given they were already hiking along a narrow trail. Storming off into the underbrush really wouldn't have the right dramatic effect.

"What I am, is right. I'm not saying that predators are better at everything, but we are better at *some* things."

She wanted to say something snarky, but she held back. They were supposed to be a team for the next few days, and that meant presenting a united front, even if she was seriously tempted to push him into the nearest snowbank.

"Haven't you noticed that most FUC agents are predators?"

"Alyce and Miranda are not predators. They're still damned good agents."

"Miranda is sabre-toothed freaking rabbit. Are you trying to tell me she's not an apex predator?"

Dammit, he had a point. "And Alyce?"

He waved a hand in dismissal. "There are exceptions to every rule. We're not talking generalities, though. We're talking about *you*."

"So I *was* fluffy and useless, but now you think I can be more?"

"I never said you were—"

"Sergei! I think I found dinner… or maybe a light snack," Annie called from up ahead.

He shot Tabi a pointed look. "This conversation is not over."

Then he was off to check out whatever Annie had found.

Reminded that she needed to be foraging, too, Tabi pushed her resentment aside and left the trail, looking for edibles. She might be cold and grumpy tonight, but by Epony's snowy mane, she would not go hungry.

7

The hike went well. They made good time and got to the first campsite before nightfall, even with several pauses to forage. Everyone had found at least one item to add to tonight's menu, an impressive feat given the conditions. He'd been even more impressed when they'd come together without prompting and decided to share everything they'd found. For now, at least, everyone was working as a team.

He'd given a demonstration on shelter building and sent the cadets off to gather materials and continue foraging while there was still light to see by. He didn't want any of them stumbling around in the woods in the dark if it could be avoided. Bast only knew what trouble they'd find. The cadets were smart and capable enough, but most of them were city-bred and had never set foot in the wilds save for occasional camping trips. Their lack of experience showed in a myriad of ways.

These were the most pampered predators he'd ever seen.

While the others were gone, he wanted to have a word with Tabi and clear the air between them. He also wanted to see how she was holding up. She was out of the library and into the wild world, now. He found her building a firepit in the middle of the clearing so they'd have a central fire for their meal.

Her pack was nearby and laid out beside it was an impressive assortment of edibles she'd managed to find during their hike. There were wild rose hips, plantain, several varieties of fern, and she'd even carved several strips of bark from some Lodgepole pines. Colour him impressed. "Not many know that's edible." He tapped the ground near the bark with his foot.

She kept arranging stones and didn't so much as look up. "It's a bit early yet for it to have a lot of nutrition, but something is better than nothing, right?"

Her tone was careful, cool, and civilized, and he had a feeling if he asked her how she was doing right now, she'd tell him she was *fine*. Not good.

He crouched beside her, putting out a hand to stop her work in hopes she'd look at him. "I think I owe you an apology."

"Mm-hmm." Her non-committal hum confirmed his theory.

"You're more than a tasty morsel. You were before your change, too. I have the utmost respect for non-predators. I just don't think that most of them are cut out to be in certain professions. They don't have what it takes."

She didn't pull away, but she wasn't looking at him,

either. "So, if I were still just a horse, you wouldn't have wanted me on this little adventure?"

"No. I'd still want you here."

She finally looked at him. "Why?"

He could almost hear the figurative ice cracking beneath his feet as he considered his next words.

"Because you've been to every one of my lectures." He touched a finger to his temple. "You're booksmart. You're organized. And I'll need your help wrangling the cadets."

"You sure it isn't because you wanted a chance to kiss me again before you left?"

"Well, that was a consideration, yeah." The words were out of his mouth before his internal filters kicked in.

"That's what I thought." She pulled her hand out from beneath his and went back to work on the firepit. "But since I'm here, I'm going to prove that you're wrong about shifters like me. You're *all* wrong."

She kept her voice low, but he didn't miss the inflection in her voice, or the subtle sweep of her hand. She'd just lumped him in with Joshua and his buddies. *Ouch.* That stung worse than the time he'd tried to steal honey from a wild bee's nest.

He got to his feet, still smarting. "And you're wrong about me. I'm a television star, Tabi. If I want female companionship, I can find it anywhere, I don't need to drag a woman into the woods to score."

She slammed the rock she held onto the ring of stones so hard it threw sparks. "Good to know you've got options. If you don't mind? I want to get this firepit sorted before it gets dark. The cadets are going to want to warm up, and I've got a feeling none of them know how to cook over an open fire."

If she froze him out any harder, he'd need to treat himself for frostbite. He nodded and moved away, because discretion was sometimes the better part of not taking a rock to the foot.

"I'll start gathering wood. Do you want a hand putting together your shelter?"

She didn't look up. "I'll manage."

He had his doubts about that.

By the time they'd served up their meagre dinner, morale had dipped lower than the air temperature. The biggest complaint had been the lack of protein, and he was already calculating odds on which of the cadets broke and ate their single ready-to-eat meal before they broke camp in the morning.

Tomorrow's lessons would include how to set snares and build fish traps. If they were lucky, they'd have protein by dinner, or maybe for breakfast the next day. By then, he was betting the only MREs left in the camp would be his. And Tabi's.

Tabi had surprised him. She'd finished building a fire ring, and moved on to building a shelter that was damned near perfect. She'd picked a cozy spot beneath a large spruce, nestled a simple bed of interwoven branches and ferns between the roots, and even created a small firepit to reflect the heat back into her sleeping area. She'd managed to find juniper berries, too, and handed them out as snacks.

"I still think we should have doubled up. More body heat that way," Joshua muttered from out of the darkness.

They were drifting back to their shelters, each of them transporting a few embers from the main blaze to start their own fires. Tomorrow he'd teach them how to start a blaze without matches, but tonight, he'd allowed them this one luxury. He wanted them to learn, and they couldn't do that if they were too cold to think clearly.

"Teamwork is one part of this exercise, but I want to see how you manage on your own, too. If you followed my instructions, then each of you should be able to stay sufficiently warm and dry tonight. If you didn't? Then tomorrow, you'll be well motivated to do better the next time we make camp."

He stayed by the fire while everyone else settled in, watching the flames die down until there was nothing left by a few glowing coals. There were eight smaller fires scattered around the area, marking the location of everyone's shelters, including his. He'd picked a spot some distance from the others. It was the only privacy he'd get until this trip was over.

Normally, he loved the solitude he could only find when he was out in the wilds, but tonight, he didn't relish the idea of spending time alone. His gaze drifted to Tabi's little abode. Her fire gave off enough light he could see she wasn't inside. She was likely foraging for more food or looking for a bush to crouch behind.

He should be doing the same thing. He got to his feet and flicked on an LED flashlight he always carried. As his night vision improved, he spotted a couple of lights moving through the trees beyond the camp, but only one was relatively close to Tabi's shelter. He picked a parallel course and made his way through the snow-covered woods, scanning the ground for anything he could use.

It took him less than a minute to catch her scent, confirming she was the source of the light dancing between the trees. Damn, she smelled good. Her personal scent was tinged with wood smoke and pine, and it was enough to make his currently non-existent tail twitch.

They'd settled into a détente of sorts, both of them working on getting the camp set up, but they were missing the easy rapport they'd had before. Apologizing, yet again, would be lamer than a three-legged goat with a bad case of gout. He could hear his father in his head already. "Women don't like weak men, son. You see one you like? You take her. Simple."

It had seemed like good advice at the time. But his old man was now on his fourth wife... or was it his fifth? Maybe it was time to try another approach. There had to be a middle ground between grovelling and knocking her on the head with a club and taking her back to his shelter for a night of naked debauchery.

He mused to himself as he gathered more firewood. It would be a cold night, and he'd need to keep the fire stoked from now until daybreak. He wouldn't admit it, but he was with Joshua about doubling up for warmth. He'd far prefer to cuddle Tabi tonight than the stones currently heating at the edge of his fire.

He was pondering how to fix things between them when all hell broke loose. There was a dull *whump*, and then a scream of shock. *Tabi*. He dropped his armload of wood, turned, and ran.

It wasn't easy to sprint through a snowy forest in the dark, and it took him longer than he liked to get back to camp. By the time he got there, Tabi wasn't the only one yelling. Someone, he thought it was Josh, was wailing like a banshee.

"Get this psycho stabby bitch away from me! Jeeze, it was a joke! That's all, just a fucking joke!"

There was a crash, followed by the sound of splintering wood, and a huge black *something* charged into the clearing, trailing the remains of a tree like streamers in its wake.

Holy Bast in a wicker basket. Was that *Tabi*?

The word unicorn had conjured visions of a delicate, ethereal creature prancing through a flower-filled meadow. He flicked his flashlight to its widest setting and finally got a good look at her.

She was a magnificent nightmare. As dark as night, with blue and purple streaks flowing through her mane and tail. She was almost two metres tall at the shoulder, built on the scale of a knight's warhorse or one of those horses from the beer commercials. Her hooves were as broad as dinner plates, and she moved with deadly power and grace.

She halted at the base of a tree and shook her head hard enough to clear the debris from her horn. Then she reared up on her back legs and slammed her hooves against the tree trunk. Her strikes gouged great chunks of wood from the bole and triggered a miniature landslide of snow from the branches.

"For fuck's sake. Help. She's gone full Stabitha," Joshua wailed.

Sergei played the light higher into the tree and spotted the traumatized cadet clinging to a branch just out of Tabi's reach.

"Shut up," he barked at Josh. "You're not helping."

Tabi squealed in fury, spun, and lashed out with both hind legs, taking an impressive chunk out of the trunk. A few more kicks like that, and either she'd shake Joshua loose or bring the whole tree crashing down. He needed to calm her before that happened.

He lowered the beam of his flashlight and walked over to her, careful to stay out of range. "Tabi. I need to know what happened, and I know you can't talk to me in that form. So, how about you shift back and let me know what this idiot did to you?"

"It was just a stupid prank," Josh protested.

"What are you, twelve? This isn't fucking summer camp. Now shut up before I decide that the easiest way to deal with this is to let Tabi skewer you so we can all get some sleep."

Tabi stamped her foot and tossed her head with a whicker that sounded suspiciously like laughter. He took that as a good sign.

"Tabi, you ready to shift back?"

She swung her head around to glower at him. *Okay then. Not ready.* He threw up his hands in a placating gesture. "Hey, beautiful. I'm not rushing you. You take as long as you need. This is the first chance I've had to see you this way, and I have to say, I'm impressed. You are gorgeous."

"Is… is he flirting with the psycho?" Guy asked in a hushed whisper. It was too dark to see him, but Sergei tracked his voice to a tree not far from Joshua.

"She's not a psycho. And shut up. I think it's romantic," Annie shot back from her spot on the far side of the clearing.

"Yeah. And you've got to admit, Ms. Willows is seriously badass like this. I mean, look at her," Peter chimed in. The lynx shifter was looking at Tabi like she was Bast herself, and Sergei had a sudden urge to swat the cub on the head and drop him in the nearest snowbank. No one was allowed to look at Tabi that way except him.

Tabi took a step back from the tree and lowered her head.

"You're breathtaking, Tabi. Truly. But I think it's time to shift back now. I want to know what happened, and you're the only one I trust to tell me the truth."

She pawed the ground once, whinnied softly, and a few seconds later, she was human again, kneeling naked in the churn of mud and snow.

He covered the ground between them in a heartbeat, already tearing off his jacket so he could wrap it around her. Modesty might not be an issue among their kind, but hypothermia was. He needed to get her bundled up and someplace warm, quickly.

One look at the remains of her shelter and he knew she wouldn't be using it again. It had collapsed under the weight of a massive dump of snow. Her fire was out and her gear buried. Joshua's prank. *Asshole.*

He covered Tabi with his coat and crouched at her side. "You okay?"

She nodded, but he could see she was already shivering.

"Arms around my neck. Hold tight. I'm getting you somewhere warm."

She threw her arms around him, clinging like a burr as he gathered her up and rose to his feet.

"I got you, beautiful."

"I wrecked the camp."

"No. That was Joshua. You brought in extra firewood and scared the crap out of that idiot in the process."

She uttered a strangled laugh. "Maybe I can get hired as a lumberjack after Director Cooper fires me."

"You're not getting fired. If anyone is leaving the academy, it'll be Josh. He doesn't have the temperament to be a FUC agent."

"He's at the top of his class, and his father's got serious pull with FUC,"

"So, he's a smart, connected asshole. Still not agent material."

"And yet they let you in," she muttered so softly he barely heard her.

"I was a smart, *charming* asshole. Plus, I never did anything that endangered someone else's life. Thanks to Josh, you've lost your gear and shelter. You're staying with me tonight."

She lifted her head and gave him a look that was equal parts gratitude, amusement, and irritation. "Is that an order?"

He considered his next words carefully and opted for honesty. "Uh... no. It's a badly worded request because I'm worried about you."

Her expression softened. "Oh. Well, in that case, I'm happy to share your shelter tonight."

He lowered her to the ground and took advantage of the darkness to do something he'd been aching to do all day. He leaned in and kissed her. He didn't care if she slapped him for it. Now she was back in his arms, he wasn't letting go until he'd gotten another taste.

The moment she rose on her toes to kiss him back, he knew—one taste wouldn't be enough.

8

The last thing she should be doing right now was kissing Sergei, but if she were honest, it was the only thing she *wanted* to do. He was arrogant, annoying, and a speciest jerk, but he was also kind, caring, and no matter how hard she tried, she kept forgetting to be mad at him. The big cat made her crazy, in more ways than one.

His kiss was as hot as a branding iron, driving away the cold and replacing it with a heat that seared her all the way to her soul. For one perfect moment, she forgot about everything else. Her humiliating loss of control, her fear that she would never be in harmony with her shifter side again, even the fact she was standing barefoot in the snow. It all faded away, leaving her breathless and clinging to the only source of warmth and strength she had. Sergei.

She had to bite back a whimper of disappointment when he broke their kiss and gave her a gentle nudge toward the shelter.

"Get inside before you freeze your bits off. There are a

couple of rocks warming by the fire. Wrap one in my sweater and curl up under the thermal blanket with it. I'll be in once I've dealt with Joshua and done what I can to enlarge the shelter." He grinned. "I've never made one for two people before."

"Once I'm warm, I can rebuild mine. I just need someone to grab my clothes and boots." The clothes she'd been wearing hadn't survived her transformation, but she had enough spares to get by. She'd have to wear everything she had left to compensate for the loss of her jacket, but she'd manage.

"Your shelter was totalled, and everything you owned is buried under the snow. You won't get any sleep at all if you try to start over now." He kissed her forehead. "Go inside. Get warm. I'll be back soon." He paused, then added. "You'll be totally safe with me. I swear. I'm not going to take advantage of you."

Being taken advantage of sounded really good to her, but she appreciated the sentiment. "I trust you."

He touched a hand to his heart. "I'm honoured." Then he turned and strode off into the darkness.

She crawled into the shelter and sighed in relief once she was nestled under his thermal blanket with the heat from the fire, taking the worst of the chill off the air. It was cramped and damp, but the air smelled of earth and fresh pine, and the makeshift mattress was surprisingly comfortable. She settled in and closed her eyes. That's when reality came crashing down on her.

All jokes aside, she would lose her job for this. Everyone at the academy had been supportive until now, but the only damage she'd done up to this point had been to minor structures and a card catalogue. This time, she'd gone after a cadet. And not just any cadet. Oh no. She'd tried to skewer the only son of a member of the Crypto-zoian council, the people who oversaw FUC.

She wrapped her arms around herself, fighting back tears of frustration. Why was it that every time she tried to step outside her comfort zone, the universe sent a wrecking ball her way? For fuck's sake, she couldn't even last a single day in the forest without losing her temper, her job, and even her damned clothes. Maybe she should give up and go back to the farm. Her family would love that. They hadn't understood her decision to leave in the first place, and since the *incident,* they'd been dropping boulder-sized hints that it was time for her to come home.

She was still adrift in a sea of self-recrimination and embarrassment when Sergei returned. "You warming up?"

"Getting there."

He crouched down at the entrance. "Annie and Pete recovered your things. The pack got enough snow inside to soak your clothing, so everyone is doing what they can to dry it all out over their fires. They rescued your thermal blanket, though." He set down her boots, and the partially emptied backpack with the silver, heat-retaining sheet tucked inside. "These will need time by the fire, but I'm glad you didn't lose the footwear."

"Me too, but it was pure luck that I'd taken them off before Joshua pulled that stupid prank and I went full Stabitha."

He frowned. "I'm not a fan of that nickname."

"That's what everyone else calls it."

"Not *it*. You. That gorgeous creature in the clearing was you, Tabi. No wonder you're having trouble connecting with your other half. Everyone keeps treating her like she's a separate entity."

She opened her mouth to argue and then stopped. Son of a seahorse, he was right. Everyone, including her, always referred to her new form by another name, like Stabitha or simply, it.

"You may have a point. But she is not gorgeous. She's homicidal."

"I've got a theory about that, too. But first, I'm going to do a little home renovation. Take down a wall, maybe build a deck." He left again, but she could tell by the crunch of his boots that he hadn't gone far.

"I vote we add a hot tub while you're at it," she called out.

The wall of greenery behind her shifted as he started rearranging things. "Might take a few days to cobble something like that together. You really want to stay out here that long?"

"Good point. How about I make us a nice cup of spruce tea instead?"

"Ugh. Don't tell anyone I said this, but I hate the way it tastes. It's like gargling my mother's floor cleaner." A gap appeared in the greenery and a silver hipflask appeared. "Good thing we've got this."

"That's contraband. And I thought you said you were using it for firestarter." She took the flask and moved out from beneath the blanket just far enough to grab her pack and looked for the tin cup they'd each been issued.

"I'm Sergei Molotov, survivalist extraordinaire. I don't

61

need accelerant to start a fire. Just give me a bit of tinder and something to strike a spark."

She privately mused the cocky cat could probably start a blaze with his mouth alone. She'd certainly felt a few sparks when he'd kissed her.

"It's still contraband."

"It's for medicinal purposes. Nerve tonic."

"I don't need nerve tonic. I'm fine." Which was a lie, but one she wasn't ready to admit to. She needed to be fine, because they had two more days to get through, and she would not to be the reason they had to cut things short.

He snorted from the other side of the barrier which was now almost a foot further back and rapidly being returned to its previous thickness. "Who said it was for you? I'm out here in the middle of the woods with fools who think they're at summer camp. Sneaking food, playing pranks. What's next? They going to TP my shelter? I need a damned drink."

"Well, if the survivalist extraordinaire needs it... I suppose that makes it okay."

He chuckled and part of the roof vanished a few seconds later. "Incoming."

She almost ducked back under the blanket, but quickly reminded herself there was no point. He'd already seen her naked, and she was going to have to reach up to grab the branches he was holding out. "More bedding?"

The night sky was strewn with more stars than she'd seen since she'd left home, their tiny light winking through the branches of the trees overhead. There was a thin sliver of moon rising, and it cast just enough light to highlight Sergei's pale blonde hair, making him easy to mark in the darkness. He blinked down at her, the gleam in his eyes more than just a reflection of the flames. "Uh. Bedding. Yeah. For our bed. For sleeping on."

"For sleeping on," she agreed, trying like hell not to blush, and failing miserably.

The temperature inside the little shelter dropped quickly now that it was open to the elements, and her next words came out accompanied by a puff of frosted breath. "We better be quick or we'll lose all the heat."

His pale eyes lit up with wry amusement. "I'm pretty sure heat is not going to be a problem for us, my little gothicus."

"You did not just call me that." She tried to glower at him, but he started handing her branches so she couldn't see his face.

"What? Gothicus is your name, yes?"

"Part of it." She added foliage to their bed, expanding it so it was large enough for both of them to sleep without touching the frozen ground.

"And you have lovely multicoloured hair." He handed her more branches.

"One more word and I'll consider putting skewered tiger on the breakfast menu."

When she looked up again, he was laughing.

She shook a finger up at him. "I am not a My Little Pony!"

"Pony? No. Little? In this form, yes, at least compared to me." He lifted the portion of interwoven greenery that formed the shelter's roof and she hunkered down so he could fit it into place again. "But I am starting to suspect that you are meant to be mine, Tabitha Willows."

She stared up at the roof as he settled it back into place and tried to wrap her head around what the crazy tiger had just said. *His?* That had a ring of possessive permanence that went way beyond flirting and toe-curling kisses.

She retreated beneath the blankets with a cup full of scotch as goosebumps that had nothing to do with the chilly temperatures chased down her spine. Why wasn't he afraid of her? Everyone else was. Hell, even she was terrified of her new form.

She tracked his footfalls as he circled around to the shelter's entrance. It was barely wide enough for him to crawl inside. He toed off his boots and removed his bulky outer jacket before easing himself past the fire, setting his gear out to dry. While he did that, she shifted over to the newly expanded part of their makeshift bed, giving him more room to move.

"You going to be okay so close to the wall? It might be colder that far from the fire."

She downed a big drink of the scotch, then took a deep breath and did the bravest thing she'd ever done in her life. She lifted the blanket in invitation. "I'll be fine. I've got you to keep me warm... don't I?"

His ice-blue eyes blazed as he prowled over to her on his hands and knees, every inch a predator. He didn't stop until they were face to face, his eyes locked on hers, his breath a warm whisper against her lips. "Yes, my beautiful Tabi, you do."

She waited for him to kiss her, but he didn't, not at

first. Instead, he drew a roughened finger down her cheek and along her jaw until he reached the point of her chin. Then, he drew her head up kissed her gently, a tender touch of the lips, nothing more.

Something deep inside her cracked at his gentleness, and she burrowed into his arms with a soft sigh that welled up from the depths of her soul.

As if that was the sign he'd been waiting for, his next kiss was hungrier. He ran possessive hands over her skin, the heat of his touch a delicious contrast to the lingering chill in her limbs.

He took the cup from her and then teased her lips with his until she opened her mouth to him, letting his tongue slip inside to dance with hers. Heat blossomed between them, hotter than a blacksmith's forge. He smelled like the forest and tasted like sin, and she wanted more.

He broke away just long enough to strip off another layer of clothes, snarling in frustration with the lack of room to move. He managed to remove his sweater before he lost patience and tore his undershirt in half and shrugged out of the tattered remains.

She had her hands on his chest before the shirt hit the ground. She needed to touch him, to feel the hard planes of his body under her fingers. She'd fantasized about him for years, and part of her still didn't believe this was really happening. The rest of her didn't care if it was real or not, so long as they got to the good part before she regained consciousness. Reality was overrated, anyway.

9

This was not what he'd intended. He'd had a firm word with himself and a carefully laid out plan. Get warm. Have some scotch. Tell Tabi his theory on why she was struggling to control her shifts. Then, snuggle up and maybe, just maybe, steal a few kisses before they fell asleep. That plan had lasted about as long as tissue paper in a hail storm.

He craved her like a junkie craved his next hit, devouring her with a single-mindedness that bordered on obsession. He was grateful she was already naked, because it was hard enough for him to get out of his clothes in the limited space of their shelter. By Bast's whiskers, he'd manage it somehow.

She had more curves than he'd imagined, her hips and belly cushioning his weight as he leaned over her, mouths locked, hands roaming over each other with fevered need.

She wanted this as much as he did.

He jerked open his pants before his erection tore through the zipper on its own, and she uttered a soft

He kissed her shoulder and she stirred, turning her head to smile up at him, her mouth still swollen from his kisses. She was flushed, glowing, and breathtakingly beautiful.

"I can't believe we just did that."

"We did. And we'll do it again, too." He leaned down to kiss her. "As many times as you say yes."

"Really?" Her smile turned devilish. "In that case, I have something to say. Yes. Yes. Yes. Yes. Oh, and also, yes."

"You're very cute when you get sassy. You should do it more often."

She pressed her lips together and managed to look prim and haughty despite the fact she was naked and mussed from their recent romp. "Librarians aren't supposed to sass. We are quite proper, thank you."

His thing for buttoned-up librarians was rapidly intensifying into a full-blown fetish. "I like you prim and proper, too, but I think you're even sexier when you're bratty."

Her smile faded. "I used to be like that more often. But then... well, you've seen what happens when I let my emotions get the best of me. I guess I've been trying to stay really grounded. No highs or lows. Just meditation and exercise so I can stay level."

He eased out of her, taking a moment to dispose of the condom and retrieve a travel pack of wet-wipes from his bag.

"That's not part of the standard kit," she commented as he handed her one of the towelettes.

"For this trip, I decided to cheat a little."

He settled in beside her so they were face to face. "I've got a theory about what triggers your shifts. I don't think your emotions are the problem at all."

"That's what they told me at the academy. I need to stay calm until I find a way to reintegrate the two parts of my self."

"The first time you changed to your new form, you were in a cage, right?"

She nodded. "They were prodding me with batons, trying to provoke a response." She grimaced. "They got more than they expected."

He stroked her cheek, remembered the scotch, and snagged the cup from its spot near the fire. He handed it to her and waited while she took a sip. "I'm sorry to make you revisit those memories, but this is important. Can you think of any time that you had an uncontrolled shift where you weren't feeling scared?"

"What? Of course. Usually I'm angry, not scared."

"Are you sure about that? That time with the card catalogue. What set you off?"

"Someone had drawn a rough sketch of a black unicorn with a sword strapped to her head and put it on my desk while I was reshelving."

"That couldn't have been all that happened." She was too controlled for that to have been the trigger.

"Do we have to talk about it?"

"Do you trust me?"

She closed her eyes and sighed. "Yes."

"Then tell me what else was going on."

"I came back to my desk and found the drawing. I balled it up and tossed it into the recycling bin."

"And?"

And while my back was turned, one of the cadets walked up and dropped a stack of books on the counter. I don't know if it was deliberate or not, but it startled me and..." She opened her eyes and stared up at him. "I was more than startled, actually. It frightened me. I didn't know anyone was there, and then, *bang!*"

"And the student with books, where were they after you changed?"

He already guessed the answer, but he wanted her to see the pattern for herself. "Behind the... oh! He saw what was happening and tried to hide behind the card catalogue."

"And tonight, you were minding your own business when you were hit with a mini-avalanche of snow that destroyed your home and buried your things. You were attacked, Tabi. I don't think it's anger that triggers your shifts at all. Your new form was born as part of a traumatic event. So now, when you feel threatened, you shift to protect yourself."

She stared at him, then huffed. "It's not fair."

His brain short-circuited, going from smug to confused so fast he could almost smell the synapses frying. "What's that?"

"You." She laid a hand on his bare chest and his confusion intensified as most of the blood he needed for thinking rushed south faster than a Canada goose at the first sign of frost.

"I'm not fair?"

"Sort of. I just think it's entirely unfair that you're hot, sexy, charming, *and* smart."

"You forgot a few. Modest. Talented..." He waggled his brows. "Good in bed."

"You're amazing in bed, but I'm pretty sure you knew that already. As for modest? Nope. Your alpha-sized ego is the only thing keeping you from claiming perfection."

He briefly considered being insulted by that, but... she wasn't wrong. "Fair enough. But I think you like my alpha-sized... everything."

She laughed again, then leaned in to kiss him. "I think I do, too."

It was silent for a few minutes, then she asked softly, "If I'm just protecting myself, what do I do to make it stop?"

"Don't try to stop it. I think that's the real problem. If you feel threatened, you should shift and fight back. Before, your default was to run from danger. Now, you're conflicted because part of you wants to stand and fight."

She settled her head on his chest and sighed. "You make it sound so obvious. Why didn't I see it before?"

"Because you thought it was about getting angry, which is understandable. Everyone else saw the problem through the same filter you did because it was the obvious answer. I'm not sure you've noticed, but I don't have many filters."

She uttered a soft little laugh that fanned across his skin. "I noticed."

"Go to sleep, my little gothicus. Tomorrow's going to be a busy day."

He stayed awake long after Tabi drifted off, enjoying

the peace of the night and the unfamiliar comfort of sharing his shelter. As he cradled his sleeping lover against his side, a quiet thought drifted through his mind. This might be what was missing from his life - someone to share the adventure.

10

She woke to the sound of birdsong and hushed voices. It took her a few seconds to remember where she was, followed by a full-body blush as she remembered who she'd spent the night with. Not that he was with her now. She was alone in their little lovenest, though judging by the freshly built up fire, Sergei hadn't been gone long.

Her spare clothes were set out on top of her backpack. He might not have the best communication skills in the world, but sometimes actions really did speak louder than words. Her stuff was dry enough to wear, so she donned her inner layers, then crawled out of the shelter and finished dressing where she had room to stand. If the rest of the camp was awake, she needed to get ready. No way she'd be the reason they fell behind schedule.

It wasn't long past dawn, and the forest still held that sense of newness that came with the rising of the sun. Colours deepened, shadows faded, and everything smelled fresh and bright. All that was missing was the smell of coffee and this morning would be perfect. She sighed and wondered if there was a Tim Horton's on the route back to the academy. She'd bribe the bus driver with everything in her bank account if he'd stop long enough for her to get a double-double coffee. A large one. Did they sell coffee in buckets?

It took her uncaffeinated brain longer than it should have to register the rising voices coming from the far side of the camp.

"When did it start?" Sergei was demanding in a voice that was pure alpha male.

"After midnight," Guy replied weakly.

"It was those fucking MRE's. They were disgusting, and now we're sick!" Joshua whined.

Tabi trudged over to find out what was going on. She didn't get far before her nose wrinkled and her stomach tried to curl in on itself. They were sick alright, and the proof of it was stinking up half the campsite. *Gross.*

Everyone was up and standing in a loose circle around Joshua and Guy's shelters without getting too close. Not even Janice was braving the stench. She stood near Annie, her expression a mix of worry and annoyance.

Sergei stood between the two miserable cadets as they sat hunched outside their shelter. "You both ate your MRE's last night?"

They nodded.

"And nothing else?"

Tabi saw the two of them exchange a look, and they both shook their heads. "Nothing."

"Then we're going to have to chuck the other meals. We can't take the risk of anyone else getting sick." He looked at the others. "Did anyone else eat theirs?"

Janice raised her hand. "Me. I had half of mine."

"And how are you feeling?"

The coyote shifter shrugged. "I'm fine. That stuff was barely edible, but I don't think it's what's making them sick."

Joshua hissed. "Janice, don't."

The pretty blonde glowered back at him. "You think the rest of the group should lose their rations because you two idiots ate crap from a gas station vending machine? I told you it was a bad idea."

"You're just pissed it had peanuts so you couldn't have any," Joshua snapped, then turned greener than the pine trees. He staggered to his feet and stumbled into the woods, groaning.

Sergei turned to Guy. "That true?"

The otter shifter nodded. He was almost as pale as the snow he was sitting on, and he looked like the faintest breeze would knock him flat.

Tabi would never admit it, but she enjoyed watching Sergei go all alpha, and she wasn't feeling the slightest bit of sympathy for the pair of idiots. Who in their right mind ate anything from a gas station vending machine?

"What was it? And how much did you eat?"

Guy was starting to look a little green around the gills. "Trail mix. Was the only thing in the machine."

"Wrapper." Sergei held out his hand.

Instead of handing it over, Guy clapped a hand over his mouth and lurched to his feet. He bolted for the woods, leaving everyone looking uneasily at each other.

Janice grunted in disgust and crossed over to Joshua's shelter, She picked a wrapper out of his scattered belongings and brought it to Sergei. "They had a few bags of this."

"And you didn't eat it because?"

"Peanut allergy. Lucky me, huh?"

"Best before date, four *years* ago?" Sergei sniffed the packet and wrinkled his nose. "Bast with bells on, they ate this? It reeks of mould."

"Snakes don't have the best sense of smell, and Guy... he'll eat anything." Jenn shrugged again and pushed her hands into her pockets.

Sergei glanced over to the woods. They could still hear the occasional moan and other, less pleasant sounds coming from the trees. He scrubbed a hand over his unshaven jaw and sighed. "I'm sorry, everyone, but we're going to need to scrub this trip and get those two back to the academy."

No one said anything. Disappointment hung heavy in the air, but everyone knew it was the right call.

"Uh, I could help them to the parking lot. I mean, it might take a few hours, but it's all downhill and the trail is easy to follow."

Everyone turned to stare at Janice in surprise. She shrugged again. "It's their own stupid fault, and they're not so sick they can't make the walk on their own. Hell, I can carry Joshua if it comes to it. He's not that big."

Someone snickered and Janice blushed and waved her hands. "Ugh, no. Not like that!! We're friends. That's all."

Pete perked up. "Yeah? I thought you two were a thing."

"Nope. I'm not with anyone." Janice crammed her

hands so deep into her pockets Tabi half expected the seams to pop.

The lynx shifter moved to stand beside Janice. "I'll go with her... uh, I mean with them. Two healthy people to help two sick ones. Makes sense, right?"

Tabi did her best to hide her smile, and Sergei just looked bemused. "I think that's very decent of you both. Definitely worth a passing mark, don't you think? Instructor Molotov?"

Sergei straightened, nodding. "Absolutely."

Janice brightened, and Pete's grin grew wider. "Thank you."

"Why don't we eat what's left from last night's foraging and break camp?" Sergei glanced at the woods. "Those two will clearly be awhile, and I'm guessing they won't want to eat when they do get back."

"We can split what's left of my MRE," Janice offered.

"And mine. No sense saving it when we'll be back to civilization in a few hours," Pete said.

The mention of food got everyone moving, and before long, the main fire was crackling, the shelters had been collapsed, the smaller fires doused, and everything was packed and ready for their departures.

They shared their meagre rations and washed it down with cups of melted snow. Joshua and Guy managed to get their gear stashed unaided, which was a good sign. They were shaky and pale, but a good night's rest in a warm bed would set them right again. Shifters healed quickly, even from self-inflicted stupidity.

Even with the addition of Sergei's spare sweater, Tabi was chilly. She'd be alright once they started moving, but last night's unplanned shift had destroyed her winter jacket, so she lingered by the large fire while Sergei stepped away to make a call. She hadn't realized he had a satellite phone with him, but she should have expected it. He was good at planning for the unexpected. He was in contact with Director Cooper, arranging transport and medical attention for the cadets headed back down the mountain.

"Hey." Janice joined her with a nod.

"Hi. It's good of you to do this, getting those two back on your own."

"Yeah, well, I don't see why everyone else should pay for their mistake." Janice blew out a breath, hesitated, and then started to talk in a rush. "Speaking of mistakes, I'm sorry about last night. Dumping that snow on you was a stupid thing to do. I thought it would only be a handful, but Joshua never knows where to draw the line."

Her first instinct was to do what she always did: deflect and minimize. Instead, she decided to be honest. "Joshua seems like the kind of person who needs to make other people feel small. Does he do it to you, too?"

Janice's lips thinned, but then she nodded.

"Then maybe it's time you found some new friends. Ones that build you up instead of tearing you down." Even as she said it, she realized that was what Sergei was doing for her. Not that anyone was tearing her down, really, but until he'd walked into her life, there hadn't been anyone in her corner, either.

Janice flashed her a tiny smile. "Like Pete?"

"Yeah. I think he's one of the good ones."

Janice glanced over at the lynx. "I think so too. So's yours."

"Mine?"

"Sergei. He is yours, right?"

She was still thinking about her answer when her mouth opened and words spilled out. "I think maybe, he is, yeah."

"Cats," Janice mused. "Who knew?"

They both laughed and bumped fists, then Janice frowned. "Where's your jacket? Oh crap, were you wearing it last night?"

"Yeah. It's gone. All I found was the zipper."

"I'm really sorry." Janice took off her jacket and held it out to her. "Take mine. You're going to need it more than I am."

"You sure?"

"I'm sure. I've got another heavy sweater I can wear over this one."

"Thanks." She took the offered garment and pulled it on.

There was a moment's silence. "By the way? Your unicorn is something else. I mean, I'd heard that's what you were, but seeing you last night? Badass."

"You think so?"

"Totally. Don't let anyone tell you differently."

"I won't." At least, she'd try. Something told her it was going to take some time for her to adjust her mindset, and everyone else's, when it came to her other form.

Sergei reappeared and Janice made herself scarce in a hurry. Almost as if she were leery of him. The thought made Tabi laugh. They were nervous of the big pussy cat.

She'd been so busy being wary of them, she hadn't noticed they felt the same way about him. She was sure there was some deep, meaningful statement to be made about everyone spending too much time worrying about what others thought... but she was too caffeine-deprived to ponder it too much right now. She'd have plenty of time for philosophy once this trip was over.

"Everything's arranged." He plucked at the sleeve of her new coat. "Janice?"

"Janice. We'll have to include that in her review."

He looked over to where the coyote shifter was carefully draping several feet of limp-looking python across her shoulders. "A lot of things are going into that review. I'm going to need your help to keep it all straight. It could take a few days to get it all written up properly."

"Days?"

"And nights. Several of them." He gave her a slow wink that made her cheeks heat. "Sound like a plan?"

"An excellent one. After all, we should be thorough about this. It's our first time acting as instructors, right?"

"Glad we're on the same page." He surprised her by leaning down to kiss her with a heat that should have melted the snow in a two-metre radius. Manes and tails, she'd never been so happy to be on the same page as someone else in her life. There was no way to guess how their story would end, but she'd happily linger in this chapter for as long as she could.

She was pretty sure the air was sizzling by the time he let her go.

They said their goodbyes and stayed put until Janice, Pete, and their sickly charges vanished down the trail.

Sergei shifted the pack on his shoulders and turned to point up the slope. "Alright, everyone. Pitter-patter, let's get at 'er. This mountain won't climb itself!"

The sun broke through the clouds, lighting the world in dazzling colour and a lens flare that would make a Hollywood director weep.

It was going to be a good day.

11

Blessed Bast, this was the kind of day he loved best. The weather was brisk but not freezing, the sun was bright, and the surrounding forest was slowly waking from its winter slumber. Even the birds seemed to know it and were singing so cheerfully it felt like they were hiking through the set of a Disney movie.

No one mentioned it, but without the brooding presence of Joshua and Guy, everyone was in a better mood. He'd have to include that in his report. He grimaced. Paperwork. *Bleh*. He wasn't kidding when he'd told Tabi it might take several days. There were things he missed about being an agent, but writing up reports was not one of them.

Tabi though...she was a constant source of surprise. He'd expected her to be out of her element, but she'd met every challenge with determination, applied what she had stored in that amazing brain of hers, and found a way to adapt. She was better at administration than he'd ever be, had managed to keep up with the cadets in every way, and one night in bed with her had quite possibly ruined him for other women.

From time to time he dropped to the back of the group just so he could watch her ass as she hiked up the trail. It would take them five or six hours to make the climb to their next campsite. Along the way, he stopped to give lessons in foraging, had them collect the makings for their fire-starting kits, and even gave a quick session in building fish traps. Though that was more theory than practical, given the stream they crossed was still full of ice.

They were nearing the halfway point when his pack started chiming. No... not his pack. The satphone inside it. He'd never actually heard the damned thing ring before. It took him a few seconds to fish the unit out and scan the brief text message. The others were safe and on their way home.

"Hey, everyone. That was a message from the Director. Your fellow cadets are on the bus and headed back to the academy."

There was a round of cheers. "Why don't we celebrate that bit of good news by taking a break for lunch? There's a clearing up ahead, and this path is used enough in the summer that you'll find a fire pit and some logs to use as seating."

That garnered another, more enthusiastic response. He didn't blame them—they were all burning more calories than they were taking in, which meant everyone was feeling perpetually hungry. It was nothing new for him, but for the cadets, it was probably a new experience.

The cadets hurried up the path, already discussing

how to divvy up the food they'd found during the morning hike and debating if it was time to share another of their MRE's. He stayed put, hoping to steal a few moments alone with Tabi. She lingered at his side, watching the others with amusement. "I think they're hungry."

"We're all hungry. I'm just not going to admit it in front of them."

"You really live like this for weeks at a time? No one sneaks you pizza between takes?"

"I wish. When I have a crew with me, they're always camped far enough away that I can't see or hear them, or smell their meals cooking. No pizza. No coffee."

"I miss coffee," Tabi admitted with a little sigh of longing.

"I miss steak. And coffee. And now I'm missing pizza, too."

Tabi looked guilty. "Sorry."

"You can make it up to—" he stopped talking. The woods had gone silent. The wrong kind of quiet that meant something was wrong.

Tabi sensed it too, he could tell by the way she stiffened, eyes wide, head moving in a slow arc to scan the surrounding woods. The woods were silent. No birds sang, and as the breeze shifted direction a new scent tickled the back of his nose. Drug store aftershave.

They weren't alone.

Instinct kicked in, and he dove for Tabi just as she did the same, the two of them tangling as they dropped to the forest floor. They hadn't hit the ground before a gunshot shattered the silence. Something whined overhead. Sonofabitch. Who were these assholes? It wasn't hunting season. Poachers, maybe?

There were exclamations and curses from the clearing up ahead.

"What the hell?" Danny bellowed.

"Get down!" Annie instructed.

It was damned good advice, because a few seconds later the woods filled with the sound of gunfire. Sergei tried to count but lost track. Either there was an entire posse of crazed poachers out here, or someone had broken about a dozen laws and brought automatic weapons into the country. Either way, they were a few miles up shit creek with no paddles. And a hole in their boat.

He looked over at Tabi. She was facedown on the ground beside him, face white, hands fisted. "You okay?"

"Should I be?" She hissed at him. "I'm pretty sure fine took a flying leap off the mountain the moment someone opened fire on us!"

"Fair point. Let me rephrase. Are you injured?"

"Oh. No." She sucked in a breath. "Sorry. First time in a firefight. So far, not a fan."

He grinned. If she could manage sarcasm and jokes right now, she would be fine. "I had thought I was done with these, being retired and all."

The gunfire quieted, but he had no doubt the second anyone moved, they'd be a target. "We need to find the others and make a plan. Stay low, move slow."

She snorted. "That's cute. The predator is trying to tell the prey how to avoid detection. Just try to remember you're the hunted, not the hunter right now. No pouncing."

"I'll keep it in mind. Oh, and this sassy thing you've got going on? Totally sexy. Don't stop. It's doing wonders for my morale." Acting like prey always bothered him, even when it was the smart thing to do.

"You're insane." She actually blushed. She was crawling through frozen mud while people shot at them, and somehow, he could still make her blush like a schoolgirl.

"It's a job requirement."

They kept up the whispered banter all the way to the clearing, and by the time they reached the others, he was more than a little in love with his little goth librarian.

To their credit, the two cadets were cool and calm. They'd taken shelter behind a fallen log and were using the tried and tested "hat on a stick" ploy to draw enemy fire.

"We've figured out the location of at least six of them," Danny informed them once they were within earshot.

"There's more out there, though, and they're not falling for the hat trick anymore. I can't get a bead on the others." Annie sniffed. "Though Ursa knows I can smell them well enough. Did they *bathe* in aftershave this morning? Ugh."

It was a good point. If they knew they were after shifters, they shouldn't be wearing any scent at all. Unless… He sampled the air again, ignoring the gag-worthy odour of Eau De Cheapskate and trying to detect what was underneath. It took him a few precious seconds, but the answer was worth it. Under the reek was a musky tang he'd know anywhere. "We've got reptile shifters after us. They can't smell for shit. They must think that drugstore drek they bathed in will stop us from recognizing what they are."

"Anyone piss off a lizard lately?" Danny quipped.

"I think MUFF sent them. Who else could it be?" Sergei was too busy working out how to get everyone safely out of range to worry too much about who was shooting at them.

Annie scowled. "Why would those MUFF wackjobs be after us?"

"Sergei's on their radar. The director gave him the heads up before we left. But I thought they were going to target your next filming location. No one knows where you are right now, so how did anyone find us way the hell out here?" Tabi asked.

Danny chimed in. "And since when do they hire gunmen? We've studied them and there's no mention of—"

Sergei cut them off with a chopping gesture. "No time. We can discuss the hows and whys when we're all safely back at the academy." He pointed to the two cadets. "Both of you can pass for local wildlife. I need you to shift and run like hell until you make it to the parking lot. Stay off the trail for the first kilometre or so in case they left someone back to watch for runners."

"What? No! Uh, I mean we should stick together, sir," Danny protested.

"I appreciate your enthusiasm, but you two aren't full-fledged agents just yet, and Director Cooper will skin me and hang my pelt on her office wall if I let anything happen to either of you. So, you're leaving."

He rummaged in his pack, looking for the satellite phone he'd crammed inside as the shooting started. When he pulled it out, he cursed. The antennae had snapped off. They had no way to call for help. "Fuck."

Danny grimaced, then shrugged. "There's a payphone over by the washrooms at the trailhead. I remember, because it's the first one I've seen in years. We can use that to contact Director Cooper through the through the FUC hotline the made us all memorize. But Sergei, sir? I think you should come with us."

"If I go with you, then they'll be sure to follow us, and we'd be sitting ducks once we got to the parking lot. I need to keep them focused on me, up here where there's plenty of room to move without following the trail. They got ahead of us because we were sticking to the main trails, so I won't use them anymore."

Annie nodded. "Makes sense, but I still think Danny has a point. MUFF aren't really the gun-toting ty—"

Sergei growled and she stopped midsentence. "You need to stick together and get to that payphone, contact the director, and report what's happening. Then, give her this message, verbatim. *Welcome to my nightmare. No more mister nice guy.* And when she asks, tell her I'll need a helicopter extraction an hour after dawn tomorrow morning. Location will be the campsite we planned to use tonight. She knows where that is."

Danny blinked at him. "Did you just use Alice Cooper song lyrics in a message to the director?"

"I'm amazed you know who that is, and yes, I did. She'll know what it means."

The moose shifter shrugged. "My parents are into

classic rock." Danny carefully stowed the satellite phone in his pack and then stripped. Annie did too, both of them stuffing their clothes into their packs. They'd need them when they reached civilization.

Sergei turned his attention to Tabi and tried not to think about the fact some of his favourite bands were now considered classics. "Tabitha, you need to go, too. You can't shift, no way to explain a unicorn running through the woods if anyone spots you, but once I distract these assholes, you need to get gone as fast as your two legs can carry you. FUC can pick you up when you get to the parking lot."

She glared at him. "I'm not going anywhere without you."

"Yes, you are. These assholes are after me. It's imperative you get as far away from me as possible."

A piercing whistle rang through the trees. The other side was getting ready to move. They were out of time.

"Go! Scatter and run." He pointed to the trees behind them.

Three seconds later, a bear and a moose charged into the woods, one with a pack in her mouth, the other with his gear dangling from one broad antler. Shots rang out, but both the cadets vanished into the trees unscathed. However, the forest remained empty of unicorns. *Dammit.*

"I told you to run," he hissed at Tabi, who hadn't moved.

"And I told you I'm not going anywhere without you. You're the one who said I needed to embrace my predator side." She folded her arms. "This is me being a predator. I'm going to fight, not run."

"You picked a hell of a time to make that call." He couldn't decide if he was more proud, annoyed, or turned on by her choice.

"So, now what?"

He kicked off his boots and dropped his jacket on top of them. There wasn't time for anything else. "Now you grab my gear and head for those trees, while I deal with these assholes. If anyone comes close to you, shift and run like hell, but try to bring the gear if you can. We're going to need it."

"But I want to fight!"

He took her by the shoulders. "You will. But you don't have the training, Tabi, and I don't have time to teach you right now. I need to thin their numbers, or we're not going to make it until reinforcements get here. Take the packs and head towards the sun. I'll find you. Now go, before they overrun this position!"

Thank Bast's fluffy tail, she didn't argue this time. She merely nodded, kissed him hard, and whispered, "Be careful."

Then she was gone, vanishing into the undergrowth with impressive stealth and speed, especially considering she was belly crawling while carrying both their gear. Once she was safely away, he shifted and bounded in the opposite direction. Gunfire shattered the silence again, and he had to duck and weave as he broke for the cover of the trees.

Despite the danger, it felt good to be in his furry form again, and he loosed a roar as he hit the treeline. Now, the tables would turn. He was in his element, a hunter...

A gun cracked, there was a thwack, a whine, and then his shoulder erupted into white-hot agony. *Son of a bitch!*

He roared again and bolted deeper into the forest, ignoring the pain that radiated down one foreleg. After the initial jolt, it settled to a low throb, and a quick glance at the injury confirmed it wasn't serious, just a graze from a ricochet. The bastards had gotten lucky, that's all. He paused to get his bearings, changing course to circle back behind them. Their luck was about to run out.

Stupid tiger telling her to run and hide. First, he was all, *be a predator, grr,* and now it was *run away and oh, take my stuff with you, while I go be a badass.*

Tabi grumbled to herself the whole time she was crawling through the mud and snow, pausing often to listen and adjust course so she didn't cross paths with the assholes trying to shoot them. Sergei might be convinced they were MUFF, but she wasn't so sure. This wasn't really their *modus operandi*. At least, not from what she understood, but there hadn't been time to explain that to Sergei. Not that he was likely to listen to her, anyway. He hadn't paid any attention to Danny earlier.

She might only be a librarian, but she'd heard plenty about all the various threats to shifterkind listening to cadets and instructors talk. Since the *incident*, she'd paid special attention in case someone dropped a hint that might help her figure out which group had kidnapped and experimented on her. All she'd been able to glean was that they were a splinter group working independently.

FUC spent a lot of time hunting down assholes like the ones that had taken her, making the world safer for shifters everywhere. But at the moment, she didn't feel very fucking safe. If this wasn't a MUFF operation, then who the hell were these people and why were they after Sergei?

She ducked behind a tree and took a moment to catch her breath, using all her senses to ascertain if she was safe. She couldn't detect anything. No footsteps, no out of place scents. There were still occasional shots being fired back the way she'd come, but nothing prolonged. She leaned back against the trunk of the tree and thought about Sergei. He was the one they were shooting at, and she'd left him back there. Alone. It didn't feel right. She'd been scared, sure, but she hadn't panicked. She should have stayed with him and found a way to help instead of running away like a scared rabbit.

That's when it dawned on her. As scared as she'd been, she hadn't shifted. Not so much as a twinge. Holy horse-shoes, she hadn't shifted!

She wanted to squeal with joy and do a happy dance, but she settled for tossing a handful of snow into the air like confetti and whispering, "Yay me!"

She was still trying to wrap her head around it all when the woods behind her exploded in a cacophony of noise. Roars, screams, and gunfire all blended into a bone-chilling concerto. She leapt to her feet, quickly shed her clothes, bundled them into her jacket, and buried the lot beneath the snow. It cost her valuable seconds, but they'd need the contents of those packs later... assuming they survived the next few minutes.

Then, prancing to keep her feet off the frozen snow as much as possible, she did something she'd been too frightened to attempt since her kidnapping. She deliberately shifted forms.

A few seconds later she was standing on four hooves, and she threw her head back to whinny in triumph. She'd done it!

Spinning on her haunches, she charged through the trees and back toward the fighting, feeling more powerful than she'd ever experienced before. If this was what Sergei had meant about embracing her new nature, then she was definitely on board with the idea.

She ducked and weaved through the forest for a few glorious minutes before slowing to a more cautious jog. She wasn't exactly built for stealth, and she couldn't spot the enemy if she was running full tilt.

A terrified wail came from over on her left, rising to an ear-piercing shriek and then ending suddenly, followed by another primal roar from Sergei. He'd taken down another one, probably killed him, but all she felt was a wave of relief that he was still alive.

A metallic click caught her attention, and she slowed to a walk as she tried to trace the sound. She caught wind of gunsmoke and aftershave and followed it back to the source. One of *them* was hiding behind a tree, his back to her, his weapon raised as he tracked something she couldn't see. There was only one target he could be aiming for. Sergei.

She closed in silently and lunged the last few metres in a sudden rush, lashing out with one hoof to strike him behind the knee. He toppled and dropped like a sack of grain. She was on him in seconds, grabbing him by one shoulder and tossing him against a nearby tree. There was a meaty thunk as his head hit the trunk. He slithered to the ground and lay still. She snorted, stomped on his gun a few times, and trotted off to find Sergei.

A shot rang out, and a dart *thwack*ed into a nearby tree. She barely had time to spot the red projectile before the air filled with gunfire and she ran like her tail was on fire, dodging through the trees and leaping over fallen logs and other obstacles.

Darts. Not bullets. That fact wandered through her head like a kitten looking for a place to nap. It was an important detail, but she was too high on adrenaline to think clearly at the moment, so she stashed it away for later.

Sergei roared again, this time in pain, and she veered toward the sound. She screamed a battle cry and charged pell-mell through the forest, breaking into a clearing. She spotted Sergei immediately. His beautifully striped coat was streaked with blood. He was moving slower than she'd expected, and she quickly realized why. Tranquil-lizer darts. He'd been hit with enough of a dose to slow him. If he took another hit, he'd go down.

Someone was speaking into a radio as she entered the fray, and his voice rose when he spotted her. "Holy shit! Primary target spotted. Repeat. Primary target spotted, and she's shifted to battle form."

"Headed back, now," someone responded.

"The bitch must have gotten past me. On my way."

"I'm getting no answer from Ripper or Flip. I thought

this was a routine extraction!" someone else shouted in near panic.

The man in the clearing stared at her, his weapon still pointed at the ground. "Guys, there is nothing routine about this. She's huge! Way bigger than we were told. Transporting these two is gonna be a major problem."

Primary target? Her? And who was this asshole to start commenting on her weight? Her vision went red as a wave of pure rage overtook her. She lowered her head and charged. The next few seconds passed in a blur of screams, fury, and bloodshed, though thankfully, the details were already fading as she trotted over to Sergei and nuzzled his injured side.

He bunted her with the broad flat of his head, and the two of them slipped out of the clearing before the others could converge on their companion's position. They didn't get more than thirty metres or so before Sergei sat down and uttered a frustrated snarl.

She shifted to her human form and dropped to her knees at his side, her hands deep in his soft fur as she checked his injuries. "We can't stay here long. How bad is it?"

He shot her a disgruntled look that made her laugh, and before she knew it she was stroking a naked man instead of a tiger. "I'm just a little woozy. That's all. Don't know why. I haven't lost that much blood."

"Did you happen to miss the fact they're shooting tranq darts at us?" Now that he was naked, it was a lot easier to see his injuries. He had a few nasty splinters of wood in his shoulder, a graze wound, and a puncture on his hip that was probably where he'd gotten a dose of tranquillizer. It was right over his hipbone, and she suspected that's what had saved him from getting a full dose.

He gave her a bleary look. "Darts?"

"I don't think these are MUFF's people. I heard them saying I was the primary target, and something about transporting us out of here." She got to her feet again, satisfied that he wasn't going to bleed out. "I think they're part of the group that took me the last time. Or at least, they've been hired by them. I hate to break it to you, Mister television star, but they're not here for you."

"Well, they're not getting either of us. Doesn't matter who they are, or who they're after. We need to finish them." He struggled to his feet, but it was clear he was in no condition to fight. Not until he'd had time to clear the drugs from his system.

She gave herself permission to take one long, lust inducing look at him before she got back to business. He was a thing of beauty as both man and beast, and later she wanted to get a better look at both forms, but this wasn't the time. She grabbed his hand and tugged. "We're not finishing anyone right now."

He followed her grudgingly, but kept looking back the way they'd come. "My dad taught me you never walked away from a fight until you were the last one standing."

"And mine taught me that he who hides then runs away, gets to live another day."

Sergei wrinkled his nose. "You want me to run and hide?"

She pulled him behind a tree and glared up at him. "I want both of us to survive until tomorrow. We're outnumbered, and you're not exactly at the top of your game, Mr. Predator. So for now, we're the hunted, not the hunters."

Shouts rang out behind them. "They found their friend," Sergei said.

"What's left of him." She tried not to think about the gooey mess she'd made of the man who'd been about to shoot Sergei, focusing instead on how far it was to where she'd hidden their packs. It was too far.

"We need to move faster than this. Naked, terrified, and unarmed really isn't working for us. Time for Plan B." She kissed him quickly and stepped back, giving herself enough room to shift.

"What are you doing?"

"Saving both of us. I'll get us to the gear. After that, you'll need to point me in the right direction. Get ready to mount up and run, cowboy." She managed a soft laugh. "And welcome to the other side of the food chain."

She shifted again and immediately felt her energy flag a little. She was going to need to recharge after this. Hell, they'd both have to, and that meant she had to get them far away from here.

She walked over to a rotting stump and stood beside it. When Sergei didn't move, she stamped her hoof and whickered.

"Don't get your tail in a twist, I'm coming." He shook his head, squared his shoulders and made his way over. He vaulted onto her back, hissing slightly as he landed, his thighs clamping her sides as he tried to avoid crushing the more delicate bits of his anatomy.

She set off, first at a walk, as she got used to the extra

weight. She'd never allowed anyone to ride her before, and she had to keep making adjustments to her balance to compensate.

After a few metres, she shifted from a walk to a canter. Sergei whooped, tangling his hands into her mane as they flew through the forest. His thighs gripped her hard, so he could shift his weight forward, his big body low over her neck to avoid the branches whipping overhead.

She spotted tracks in the snow, the footprints too small to be anyone but her own. She was on the right trail! They'd be able to recover their gear and then dash off again.

It only took a few minutes to find the spot, and she slowed to a walk, then stopped in front of the tree, pawing the ground to show him where their stuff was buried. He pulled out the packs, dressed, and then remounted, using more care this time.

"I have to admit, this is not how I imagined my first time riding you bareback would go."

She snorted and swung her head round to glare at him. She might not be able to speak, but she thought he'd get the point. Now was not the time for sex jokes.

He grinned and patted her neck. "Sorry, I couldn't resist. Head in the same direction as before. Try to avoid the snow where you can—no sense leaving them a trail to follow. We're going to stay far from the main trails. It'll make it harder for them to guess where we're going."

She noted he didn't tell *her* where they were going, either. But what the hell, after the day they'd had, what was one more surprise?

13

If it wasn't for the fact he was woozy and hurting, Sergei would be having the time of his life rocketing through the woods astride what he'd heard one of them call Tabi's battle form. He grinned. *Battle-corn*, more like. Yeah. He liked the sound of that. When they got back to the academy, he'd make sure the legend of the battle-corn was planted. By the time he left, they'd have forgotten about calling her Stabitha.

An ache filled his chest, vague but persistent. He didn't like the idea of leaving. He'd agreed to this whole insane trip so he could steal a few more days with her, and even though they were running for their damned lives, he wasn't sorry about the choice he'd made. She was worth it.

His joy in their wild escape faded as he realized that while he had no regrets, Tabi likely had a list of them. She'd come on this trip hoping for a little adventure and romance. Instead, she had risked her life to save his sorry ass from a bunch of cut-rate mercenaries. He was supposed to be helping *her*, for fuck's sake. Not the other way around.

He leaned to one side to avoid a branch, his reactions slowed by the drugs in his system and his balance fucked up by the two packs he had slung over his shoulders.

It stung him to admit she'd been right about that, too. He was in no condition to fight right now. If his father could see him now, he'd roar in horror. Running and hiding were not the Molotov way. Nor was getting your tail pulled out of the fire by a female, for that matter. Even if she was the most magnificent woman he'd ever met.

By the time they arrived at their destination, they were both more than ready to stop. He hadn't done a lot of horseback riding in his life, and none of it had been bareback. His legs ached and there were parts of his anatomy that weren't going to be speaking to him for quite some time, but at least the drugs were fading from his system and he could think clearly again.

He dismounted, setting aside the packs as Tabi shifted back to her human form. She looked as wrung out as he felt, and it was the most natural thing in the world to walk over and cuddle her close against his chest. They leaned on each other in silence, and when she started to shiver he scooped her into his arms rather than let her go.

"I should get dressed. Then I need to check on your injuries. I know you'll heal on your own, but if I can get the splinters out and everything cleaned up, you'll recover faster." She gasped. "Hell, you're hurt. You shouldn't be carrying me! Put me down, right now."

He shook his head. "No. Don't want to."

"You have to."

That made him smile. "You are not the boss of me. And as much as I'm looking forward to playing nurse and wounded warrior, there's something I want to show you, first."

She looked around. "Trees, rocks... Oh, and over there, I see rocks and trees."

"For the record, sassy and naked is even sexier than straight up sass." He lifted her higher, ignoring the twinge in his shoulder. She was probably right about the splinters. He could feel them snagging on the fabric of his shirt, but they could wait a few more minutes. He'd chosen this place for a reason, and he wanted her to see it. He got his bearings, mentally realigning himself with the maps he'd seen of this area. He hadn't been here before, but he'd spoken to a couple of local guides about the area while he was planning the week-long outings with the FUC agents. They'd all mentioned this spot. It was off the main trails and only known to a few locals, which was perfect, but he'd avoided bringing anyone here for the very reason they'd all recommended it to him. The last thing he wanted to do was bring the agents to their very own private hot spring.

It only took a few steps before he could smell he was headed in the right direction, and Tabi perked up the moment she caught a whiff of sulphur and other minerals. "Is that..." she trailed off as they both spotted a gleam of water through the trees.

"Your bath awaits, milady."

Tabi uttered a soft squeal of delight. "Hot springs! This is why you didn't tell me where we were going?"

"I didn't want you to be disappointed if we had to keep

going. I wasn't sure how long it would take to lose them, but you did a hell of a job following my directions. Between the game trails where we hid your tracks among other animals and the stream we followed, I think we're safe."

She turned her head to check the position of the sun, but not before he caught the first glow of a pleased flush blooming on her cheeks. "We've got a couple of hours of daylight left. We can move on if we need to."

"So we rest up, grab some food, and reassess an hour or so before sundown. Once it's dark, we should be good until morning. If they were moving at night, they'd have caught up to us sooner. They followed us that first day and got the jump on us because we broke camp late."

"You're saying they got lucky?"

"I'm saying this is what I get for sticking to the safe routes." It was six kinds of irony that if he'd taken the cadets into the riskier areas, they'd be in less trouble than they were now. Then again, he and Tabi were the only ones currently in danger. Annie and Danny could make the run in good time in their animal forms, and none of the mercs appeared to have gone after them.

"You couldn't have known we were being tracked. None of this is your fault, it's mine. If I hadn't come along, you'd all have been fine."

"I wouldn't be out here if you hadn't said yes." The confession was past his lips before his filters detected the lapse.

"What do you mean?" She wriggled in his arms. "Dammit, put me down and answer the question."

"I thought we already established that I wasn't putting

you down until you saw your surprise." He was only a few steps away from the edge of the trees now and the breeze blowing past them was as warm as a spring afternoon.

"Stubborn tiger."

"Yep."

"But this is still my fault. If I hadn't come on this trip, you wouldn't be hurt. We'd all be safe right now."

He stopped walking and raised her until they were eye-to-eye. "They were waiting for you to leave the grounds, Tabi. Watching for who knows how long. If you hadn't left with me, they'd have grabbed you the next time you drove out those gates."

She paled. "I haven't left the academy grounds in ages. I gave up my apartment and put my things in storage right after the kidnapping. Can you imagine what would happen if I lost my temper and shifted somewhere the public would see me? It would be a catastrophe for shifters everywhere."

"And as much as it hurts my heart to know you've been stuck on the grounds all this time, I'm glad, too. It kept you safe."

She trembled slightly and burrowed deeper into his embrace. "They're never going to let me go, are they?"

"Between us, we've already put down half the team they sent. It's clear they had no idea who they were hunting, or how dangerous you were. They're a third rate crew operating on second-hand intel. Once FUC gets here, this will all be over fast." He kissed the tip of her nose, carried her out of the woods and into a little slice of paradise.

Smooth rounded rocks lined the sides of the stream, and someone had used them to create a bathing pool about the size of a standard hot tub. The stones' dark grey colour changed to an unearthly blue-green where the water touched them. Even from where he stood, he could see the soft undulation of the algae that clung to the rocks and gave the spring it's odd colouring. Evergreens framed the little clearing, their trunks and branches twisted by the winds and somewhat stunted by the lack of rich soil.

Birds sang, the afternoon sun shone down with surprising strength, and for a moment, he let himself forget their dire circumstances and just enjoy the moment.

Tabi gestured to the spring. "This is lovely. How did you know it was here?"

"Several locals told me how to find this place, I just didn't think I'd get a chance to see it." He set her down gently, aware that as much as he'd like to walk straight into the water, that wasn't a good idea given he was fully dressed. Plus, he hadn't checked the temperature of the spring yet. He was banged up enough already, no need to risk boiling his favourite body parts. If the universe would cut him just a little slack, he might get to use those bits later.

She padded over to the water and crouched, holding her hand a few centimetres above the surface. "Warm, but not insanely hot. Do you think it's safe?"

"Just don't dunk your head."

She shot him a confused look. "Why not?"

"Brain-eating amoebas." He toed off his boots, more than ready to soak in the heat of the pool.

She leaned back from the water. "Tell me you're kidding."

"Nope. They go up your nose and into your brain. Keep your face above the water and you'll be fine. And before you ask, the nose is the only access point you need to worry about."

Tabi grimaced. "Ew. I'm starting to remember why I like living in a city. The only thing trying to kill you there are other people."

"People are a problem everywhere. Which is why I like to be where there aren't any." He nodded to the water. "You've got to be chilly. Get in and warm up."

"If something grabs me and pulls me under, you're coming to save me, right?"

"Always." And by Bast's whiskers, he meant it.

She dipped a toe into the water and uttered a blissful sigh. He stood and watched as she eased herself carefully into the pool and then stretched out on her back, floating in the heated water. "The rocks are really slippery. Be careful."

He shucked the rest of his clothes and hurried to join her. One thing running and hiding had going for it, it gave him more time alone with Tabi. Score one for the prey side of the food chain. Still, this lull may not last long, and he wanted to make the most of it. He had barely settled into the water before she floated over to him, her cheeks already flushed with heat.

She straddled his lap, which was about the best thing that had happened to him all day, and then she ruined the moment by running her fingers along the cluster of splinters still buried in his shoulder. His body had already pushed some of them out on its own, but the rest were still stuck in and damned uncomfortable. "I need to remove these. They've got to be hurting you."

"I can think of a few things that would distract me from any and all discomfort." He rocked his hips, bumping his cock against her inner thigh. "Wanna help take my mind off my boo-boos?"

She flashed him a sexy little smile. "How about we do a little of both? You get a kiss for every one I remove."

"Just a kiss?"

"Let me do them all without any more complaining, and I'll sweeten the pot." She tried to waggle her brows at him, but she was laughing too hard to get it right. It was the sweetest, sexiest thing he'd ever seen. He drew her in for a kiss that burned hotter than the volcanically heated water they were bathing in, and something deep inside clicked into place. There was no fanfare, no explosion of fireworks, but at that moment, he knew.

She was the one.

No doubts. No questions. She was his, and by Bast's fluffy fucking tail, he would die before he let anything happen to her.

His moment of revelation was cut short by a brief moment of pain, and he broke the kiss to glance down at his shoulder. The little minx had pulled out one of the splinters.

"Cheater."

Her smile was as innocent as a newborn kitten's. "It worked, didn't it? And no complaining, or the deal is off."

He pressed his lips together and winked. "Mhmm."

"Good kitty." She finished quickly, her fingers deft but gentle. She smoothed a wet hand over the injured area when she was finished and bowed her head to dust several tender kisses to the spot. "Boo-boos all better or will be soon."

"I have got to say, naked nursing is a vast improvement over the usual kind. You're hired."

"Yeah?"

He slid a hand into her hair and pulled her in for another kiss before he did something stupid, like tell her he was planning on making it a lifetime contract. He'd save that bit of info for another day, one when they weren't trying to avoid a lifetime spent as lab rats for some lunatic band of psychotic pseudo-scientists.

14

Tabi was more than happy to give in to the mind-melting attraction between them. She needed a distraction right now, so she didn't think about the fact she'd hurt people today. Granted, they were assholes that were trying to hurt her, but she still didn't feel good about it.

When Sergei kissed her, that all went away. The fear, the guilt, everything awful faded, and all that was left was a heady blend of joy, need, and ecstasy. It was all the more intense because she knew it couldn't last. They'd get through this, and when they did, he'd be gone. All she'd have was the memory of these wild, wonderful moments.

The heat of the water was a balm, soothing her body even as Sergei's touch did the same to her soul. Together, the effect was almost magical. His mouth claimed hers in an all-consuming kiss and she looped her arms around his neck, anchoring them together.

Strong hands gripped her hips, guiding her down until their bodies were pressed tighter from shoulder to groin.

He shifted forward, and before she knew what he was up to, he had coaxed her legs to wrap around his hips.

"Here?" She asked, her voice so breathy and low she barely recognized it.

"Here is a lot warmer than out there."

"Excellent point." She wriggled against him. "And this way, you're the one dealing with the rocks."

"A sacrifice I'm more than happy to make."

He moved to kiss her again, but she laid a hand on his cheek, stopping him. "I don't want you to sacrifice anything for me. Just make the world go away for a little while, please?"

"Whatever you need, Tabi. It would be my honour to provide it." There was something in his tone that sent a delicious thrill through her. She didn't know what it was, but part of her reacted like she'd just been offered a triple whip mocha with three shots of espresso. "Then once this is over, I'd like a fudge sundae and coffee. Lots of coffee. In bed."

"Do I get to be in this bed?"

"Will you have coffee?"

"Anything you want, sweetheart."

"Then yes, you're invited to join me in this theoretical bed."

"Good."

He slid his hand between their bodies and toyed with her clit as his tongue danced with hers. She ground herself against his calloused fingers, loving the way his rough skin added another layer of sensation to what was an already mind-blowing experience. Her mother had always told her to find a man who was good with his hands. *Oh, how right she was about that.*

Their lovemaking was more intimate this time. Face to face, limbs tangled, every sense was attuned to his presence. The rasp of his beard on her cheek, the woodsy scent that clung to his skin, the taste of his kisses, the feel of his hands on her body. True to his word, he made her forget about everything but him.

He took her to the peaks of pleasure, then sent her tumbling into an orgasm that tore through her with an intensity that stole her breath away in a low cry he muffled with a kiss. She was still caught up in the aftershocks when he lifted her a few inches higher, holding her there as he stared up into her eyes. "If you tell me to go get a condom, I will, but I don't want there to be anything between us this time. The choice is yours."

"Don't go." It wasn't what she'd intended to say. 'Take me tiger,' would have been clearer and less loaded with things she had no business thinking, never mind putting into words. She froze and waited for his reaction. To her relief, all he did was grin and draw her down the crown of his cock. "How about I make us both come, instead?"

"Yes, please." She didn't wait for him to move. Instead, she flexed her legs, pulling them together, their bodies merging with a suddenness that made her gasp and him groan.

Her inner walls gripped him tight and his body arched beneath hers as he thrust deep.

"Mine." He growled the single word so softly she couldn't be sure she'd heard it at all. After that, neither of them spoke again. There was no need. Every touch was a promise, every kiss filled with passion. Need flowed between them, fueling every thrust and counter, the two of them in perfect synch.

When he threw back his head, she muffled her cries against his neck, her nails raking the tops of his shoulders as her control slipped away a little at a time, pushing her closer to her breaking point.

He whispered her name, his lips brushing her ear, and left a trail of butterfly kisses down the side of her throat. His cock thickened and jerked inside her, and then, he bit her. The pain was minor, but it blended with her pleasure, triggering a release that unfurled with slow, exquisite perfection. Another thrust and he was emptying himself inside her, his groans muffled against her skin.

She slumped against him, as limp as an overcooked noodle and he cradled her against him as their heartbeats slowed and the details of the world outside the two of them gradually returned.

"You bit me. I didn't know I liked that," she whispered.

"No, sweetheart, I *marked* you. And I liked it, too." His voice was soft, but the effect of his words hit her like a shout.

"Haha, funny. Marking is for mates. Not to mention, it's sort of barbaric."

He nuzzled the tender spot on her throat. "And you liked it."

"But we're not..." she lifted her head so she could see him. "Are we?"

He raised his head, and there was no mistaking the primal gleam in his ice-blue eyes. "Did you miss the part where I said you were mine?"

"Saying something doesn't make it true. If it did, politicians would be changing reality every thirty seconds."

His eyes crinkled with silent laughter. "This is true."

"And this is not the Dark Ages. You don't go around biting girls just because you like them." Not that she didn't like the idea of having something serious with Sergei. Manes and tails, she was all for it, but consent was a thing, and communication was clearly not one of his strengths.

"You said you liked it." His eyes darkened and a muscle in his jaw ticked.

"I did. But you still should have asked, first."

He grunted in male frustration but didn't actually say anything. Hurt and confused, Tabi retreated, moving out of his lap to drift to another part of the pool. "So, now what do we do?" She didn't know if she was asking about their relationship, the fact they were still being hunted, or both.

Sergei rose out of the water, and she got a look at his injured hip. It was healing fast, which was good to see. "Now, I take a quick look around and make sure we're alone. If we're in the clear, then we can set up here for the night. The rendezvous point is far enough away we'll need to get started two hours before daybreak to get there on time. It's not going to be an easy run, but we'll make it."

He gave her a ghost of a smile and she thought she saw a flicker of approval in his eyes, but both were gone a bare second later. "Gather up our gear and stay out of sight until I get back."

She didn't even have time to answer before he shifted and bounded off, leaving her alone in the spring.

She huffed. "Wait until I do up my report on you, Sergei Molotov. Good leader, but lacks communication skills and does not share plans with others. Also, he's sexist, speciest, and... and... Argh!" She hit the water hard enough to send a spray arcing onto the shore. She made her way out of the pool with care, then stomped across the rocks to Sergei's clothes. "In the middle of nowhere, on the run, and somehow I am still picking up after a man. What the fuck is wrong with me?"

She leaned down, already shivering, and a new plan came to mind. Why carry his clothes when she could wear them? She pulled on the loose-fitting sweat pants and shirt, tying knots in both to improve their fit. Then she stepped into his too-big shoes and made her way back to their gear, thankful she didn't have to do it barefoot.

She gathered up their things and brought it all back to the spring. It was warmer there, and the spring was shielded from view by the trees. She changed into her own clothes and settled under one of the larger pines. Her senses hummed as she tried to sort through every sight, sound, and scent, searching for any trace of Sergei or the assholes hunting them.

Who were they? When she got back to the academy, she'd be demanding answers to that question and a host of others. She'd let herself be reassured by FUC's promises that the threat was gone, but clearly, they'd been wrong. Not only was she still in danger, but if the jerks following her figured out that the academy was more than it pretended to be, the ones who had taken her might decide to raid the place and take every shifter they could find. She hunched deeper into her borrowed jacket. She'd have to leave. Give up her job and get FUC's help to give her a new identity.

She sniffled and gritted her teeth, willing herself not to cry. This wasn't the time. She could blubber and eat vast quantities of ice cream after this was over. Vats of ice cream would be needed to build up her courage before she told her parents they'd been right all along. Looking for excitement and adventure had brought her nothing but trouble. She rubbed the tender spot on her neck again. Trouble, and an arrogant tiger who lived a life of non-stop adventure. How did he think she could ever be part of a life like that?

15

Sergei stalked through the woods in silence, but inside his head, things were noisy as hell. What had he been thinking, marking Tabi? And why wasn't she happy about it? Granted, it was a serious declaration of intent, but any other woman he'd been with would have been screaming yes and planning the wedding before she'd finished her orgasm. But no... not Tabi.

He growled and slashed his claws down the bark of a tree, shredding it. Tabi frustrated the fuck out of him. She was smart, sexy, and she bent his brain worse than that one time he'd eaten the wrong mushrooms and wound up wandering the woods for a few hours talking to trees and picking a fight with his own reflection in a lake.

Tail lashing, he continued his patrol, almost resenting the fact the area was clear and there was no one he could tear apart. He wove through the forest, taking care to obscure his tracks as much as possible. When he was satisfied they weren't being followed, he circled back toward the hot spring. The temperature was already dropping, and the skies were clear, which meant it was going to be a long, cold night. They couldn't risk a fire, either. The light and scent of smoke would make it too easy to find them.

Tabi knew he was there before he broke cover, an impressive feat considering he'd been doing his best to be stealthy. She was continuously amazing and confounding him. A fact that made him question his sanity. Why the hell did he want a woman who drove him to distraction?

The answer came to him as clearly as if Bast herself had howled it in his ear. Because life with her would never be boring. She was a new adventure, one that could last the rest of his life. *Well, fuck.*

She watched him from the shadows beneath the trees where she'd been hiding, her expression wary, though he could see she was relieved to see him, too.

He shifted to human form and pulled on his clothes as he asked, "All quiet?" Lame as it was, it was the only safe question he could think of.

"Yes. Anything out there besides trees and birds?"

"All clear. I think we're good to set up camp and spend the night right here."

She nodded. "Warmer here, and we'd hear anyone coming this way. I didn't notice before, but we're in a small gully, and the rocky outcroppings carry sound well."

To his chagrin, he realized he hadn't noticed either. Then again, they'd both been distracted by other things. Sexy, glorious things that he'd really like to spend all night doing. Instead, he suspected they'd have to do one of his least favourite things—talk. Talking was a bit tricky, though, when the other person was doing their best to avoid you.

She headed off while he was still trying to come up with an opening line. "I'll start gathering branches so we've got something to sleep on."

And so it went. For the next hour, they worked in relative silence and got their camp organized. At least she didn't seem to mind the fact he was building a shelter for two instead of separate ones for each of them. She made a bed for them inside the shelter, layering their extra clothes on top for comfort and warmth. Then she'd gone out and retrieved fresh, clean snow by the cupful, melting it by the spring and transferring the water into their canteens.

They worked so well together they barely said more than a few words, which was both amazing and annoying as hell. Their synergy was just one more sign they were meant to be together, but it was making it hard to start a conversation.

They broke out their MREs for dinner. It wasn't until he opened his packet of chicken and pasta that he realized that in all the excitement, they'd missed lunch. "After the day we've had, we're going to need more calories than this."

She looked up from her meal. "It's getting dark, but I could see if I could find more juniper berries."

He wrinkled his nose. "Nope. Screw foraging for food. We've got something better."

Tabi cocked her head, the few bits of hair that had

escaped her braid falling across her face as she did so. "Did you cheat again?"

"I didn't, but if you'll recall, I did catch some of the others trying to smuggle chocolate bars. I had forgotten about them until now."

There was no missing the way she perked up at the mention of chocolate. "Dessert?"

"There's a few. I think we can have dessert and set aside one for breakfast."

"I would happily kill for chocolate. Or coffee. Or both. My parents would be horrified at what I've become."

"What? Why?"

"When I mentioned I was raised in a shifter commune? I wasn't exaggerating. My parents are vegan, pacifist tree-huggers still sad they were born a few decades too late to be flower-children." She pointed to her meal. "I left home and became a meat-eating, caffeine addicted, processed food eating member of the establishment. I even get my pay cheque from the Cryptozoian council."

He snorted. "Whereas my folks would be thrilled if I'd taken that route."

It was her turn to look surprised. "But you're a television star!"

He shrugged. "Which doesn't impress either of them. My mom thinks I take too many chances and need to settle down with a nice, gentle woman who will take care of me and convince me to stay home. My dad thinks I don't take nearly enough risks on the show and he's embarrassed he raised such a wimp."

"Well, I think they're both wrong. They must fight about you a lot if they feel so differently about their son."

He answered without thinking. "Oh, they used to fight about anything and everything, which is why they've been divorced since I was ten."

She gaped. "Your parents are *divorced*?"

That reaction was why he didn't usually talk about his folks. Shifters weren't much for divorce. It happened, but it wasn't common. "Mom's remarried and a happy home-maker. I think my dad is on wife number four now. To be honest, I've lost track. We don't talk much."

"Well, that explains a few things."

He bristled. "What does that mean?"

She smiled, her eyes gleaming with mischief. "Wisdom is more valued when it comes at a price. Chocolate, please."

"This better be some deeply insightful wisdom." He rummaged in his pack until he found dessert and held out the bars for her to choose from.

"Yes! There's a Coffee Crisp! I can appease two cravings at once." She gleefully took the offered candy bar and tore the wrapper off.

Her next words came out around a mouthful of chocolate. "We're all a product of our upbringing. Even if we rebel, we can't escape it. Your parents broke up when you were still a kid, which is bound to leave you with some emotional scars. Add in the fact it sounds like your dad doesn't have a lot of respect for relationships, or you, for that matter. You were a FUC agent. You take risks every day. He should be proud of you."

"But what does that explain, exactly?"

She gave him a knowing look. "Why you're not good at

communicating what you're thinking. You're an only child, right?"

He nodded.

"Only child. Parents divorced when you were young, but not so young you don't remember what they were like together. Add in the fact you're trying to be different from them and prove yourself at the same time?" She spread her hands out in front of her. "Voila. Sergei Molotov, determined loner and solo adventurer. You against the world."

She had a point. Several, in fact. His need to go his own way had been part of the reason he left FUC, and while he communicated well with his crew, they had long since gotten to the point he didn't need to say much to them. They knew their jobs and did them well.

Tabi took another nibble of chocolate, then added. "And your mother sounds nice, but if she thinks you are going to settle down with a sweet caretaker of a wife, she really doesn't know you very well."

He claimed an Aero bar for himself and put the last of the candy aside for their breakfast. "So, who do you see me settling down with, then?"

"Someone like you. She'll need to be confident and capable with an adventurer's spirit. You need a partner, not a homemaker." Tabi waved around them. "This is not a life for someone who wants to stay home and bake cookies."

"I know someone like that. She's got a sharp mind and is probably more capable than I am when it comes to organizing things. She's a brave, sexy as hell unicorn shifter, and I think she'd make a hell of a partner."

She blinked at him, her mouth opening and closing several times before she managed to say anything. "I'm nothing like that."

"Says the woman who survived being kidnapped and experimented on. Who has coped with a survival training trip that's turned into the plot of a bad movie without complaint. Hell, you've even managed to crack jokes while under fire. You are everything I just described, Tabi. All of that, and more."

He wasn't good at heartfelt conversations. She'd been right about that, but he thought he'd done pretty well - until she started crying.

Fuck.

He moved to sit beside her, and when she leaned into him, tears still streaming down her face, he did the only thing he could think of. He stretched out his legs and lifted her onto his lap. "Hey, whatever I said to upset you, I'm sorry."

"It's not you. It's me. I..." she snuffled and buried her face in his chest.

Crap. Those words were always bad news. "You're what, my little gothicus?"

She huffed softly. "You have to stop calling me that."

"I don't want to stop. So, how about you explain to me why you're so convinced that you *aren't* mine."

"It can't work between us. Every time I try to leave my comfort zone even the slightest bit, I land smack in the middle of something like this. I'm done trying. If we get out of here, I'm going to ask FUC to put me in some kind of witness relocation program. They have those, right? It's the only way I can protect everyone I care about. I need to disappear until they are a hundred percent sure the threat is gone."

He wanted to roar his frustration to the darkening sky. If she went into hiding, he'd never see her again. Worse, she wouldn't have any chance at a real life. She'd be in a cage built of fear and uncertainty instead of metal, but it would still be a cage. "They have those, but... it's not an easy way to live. I don't think you'd be happy."

She sighed. "Probably not. But I would be alive, and maybe it won't have to be for very long."

He hated this plan more every second, but for the moment, he didn't have a better suggestion. He was going to come up with one, though, because letting her vanish from his life was not happening. "I thought you were done running?"

She gave him a sad, sweet smile that tore into his soul. "I did too. But how do I fight an enemy who knows everything about me, when I don't even know who they are?"

"We'll find a way."

She didn't reply. They stayed curled up together, watching the sunset paint the sky in ever darkening colours. Pinks and golds that faded to deep crimson and purple, and as the light faded, the sounds of the forest slowly died away to near silence. The spring burbled softly, the trees creaked and groaned in a light wind, but it was as close to true silence as this part of the world ever got.

Usually he was alone during the transition from day to night, and it always made him acutely aware of his solitary life. Not tonight. He had Tabi with him, and that changed everything. He wasn't lonely at all. He felt complete and at peace. There wasn't a chance in hell he'd let go of that feeling, or her.

16

Every time she thought she had him figured out, Sergei surprised her by doing the unexpected. When she'd cracked and started to cry, she thought he'd react with disdain or at least disinterest. Instead, he'd done his best to make her feel better. Hell, he'd even apologized, even though he had no idea why she was crying.

Then, when she'd told him her plans and why it couldn't work between them, he'd tightened his arms around her and told her they'd find a way to fix things, like that was the end of it and the world was just going to have to bend to his will. She smiled to herself. Given who he was? That's probably exactly what he expected to happen, and who knew, maybe it would.

She understood him a little better after their talk. She'd always assumed that someone with his confidence and status had the full support of a strong family. Instead, he was forging his own path, and in some ways, he was even more alone than she was. Her parents supported her, even if they didn't understand her choices. He barely spoke to his. He was still arrogant and pushy, but she was starting to understand why, and if she was honest with herself, she liked him that way. Hell, she liked him, period.

As night fell, she spotted a glimmer in the trees. It had to be several kilometres away, but it looked like... "I think our asshole friends built a fire."

Sergei tensed. "Where?"

She pointed. "There. See it? Or am I imagining things?"

He rumbled deep in his chest. "You are not seeing things. Thank Bast that whoever is after you can't afford a better class of SCUMBAG."

It was another name she recognized from her time at the academy, but since it was also an appropriate insult for that group, she had to clarify. "Are you calling them scum, or do you think they're from the Shifter Collective of Underground Mercs, Bombmakers, Anarchists, and Gunmen?"

"Both, but mostly the latter. And from what we've seen, they're clearly from the discount rack, which is something we can be grateful for."

She heard the anger in his voice and steeled herself for what she expected would come next. "You want to go after them, don't you?"

He growled. "Of course I do, but it's not the smart move. We're not back to full strength, for one thing. At least now we know where they are. Near as I can tell, they're following the same trail we were before they ambushed us."

"Which means they're between us and the rendezvous site, right?"

She expected him to dismiss her question with a casual answer, but this time, he didn't. "There's the fire, right?"

"Mm-hmm."

He pointed into the night sky, where a million stars were now shining like tiny motes in the darkness. "See that large star? The one that's almost straight up from the campfire?"

It took her a second, but she found it. "Okay, I see it."

"Good. Now, draw a straight line to the right until you see a group of stars that looks a bit like a rabbit. Big ears above eyes and nose. Then, swing your gaze down until you find another cluster of stars that don't really look like anything, but it's a little brighter than anything else around it."

"Okay."

"Below that is the spot we need to reach tomorrow morning. I'll show you the landmarks in the morning so you'll be able to find it on your own."

"My own?"

"If things get bad, I want you to hightail your ass out of there."

"Leave the fighting to the real predator?" She'd had a taste of what it meant to be on that side of the food chain, and she hadn't liked it, but she liked the idea of running away and leaving Sergei to fight alone even less.

"You are a real predator, and a badass battle-corn. I just don't want you to get hurt, or worse, hurting someone else. I know what kind of toll that takes, and I'm sorry I fucked up so badly you had to come and haul my ass out of there."

"I've never attacked intentionally before. I mean, I knew what I was doing. Not like the other times." She swallowed hard. "And today, I chose to kill someone." That knowledge would haunt her for the rest of her life, but it didn't change anything. She'd do it again if it meant protecting Sergei.

"I know." He wrapped his arms even tighter around her and rocked her in his arms. "And that's on me. I'm sorry."

This time, she didn't fight the tears. She let them fall, and it felt good. At least it was too dark for him to see her red, swollen eyes.

"You were magnificent, you know."

She laughed through her tears. "Only you would think so. Besides, you were loopy on tranquilizers. Your judgement is not to be trusted."

"I remember the moment you charged into the clearing. Beautiful. Dangerous. And mad as hell that someone was trying to hurt me." He smoothed a few strands of hair back from her face. "I don't doubt your abilities for a second, Tabi. Not as prey, or predator. I'm sorry I ever called you fluffy."

She snorted. "So you should be."

"As amazing as you are, I'm still going to worry about you, though. Because I will lose my fucking mind if something happened to you."

She leaned into his touch, lifting her hand to cover his. "I might regret admitting this, but I feel the same way about you."

He leaned in to kiss her and managed to mash their noses together instead. He got it right the second try, but then they were both laughing a little, and the night didn't seem so dark anymore.

"If we get out of here—" He cut her off with another soft kiss. It was sweet, and tender, and it warmed her better than the hot meal they'd just eaten. He tasted of chocolate, and she belated remembered they hadn't finished their deserts, though if she had to choose, she'd take more of his kisses over chocolate any day. Not that she was telling him that. His ego didn't need that information.

"When we get out of here," he corrected her eventually, but by then her head was whirling and she'd almost forgotten what she'd been talking about.

"Okay. *When* we get out of here, will you help me get answers out of FUC?"

A low, satisfied rumble rose from his chest. "It would be my pleasure."

"Thank you." If she had Sergei on her side, maybe she'd finally get hard facts instead of vague statements. Plus, it would be nice to have someone in her corner. She snuggled into his arms, feeling safer than she had any right to be considering their situation. It was more than a little nuts, but she couldn't deny the truth - the big, pushy tiger made her feel better about everything, even when he was driving her crazy.

She shut her eyes and tried to ignore the little voice in the back of her mind that kept whispering words she wasn't ready to hear. Falling for Sergei wasn't just a bad idea, it was a waltz off the cliffs of insanity and into an ocean of heartache... wasn't it?

They stayed like that, eating chocolate, sharing kisses,

and staring up into the breathtaking beauty of the night sky until the cold crept into their bones.

"You know, we have this lovely hot spring. Maybe we should use it to warm up before we go to bed," she suggested.

"Brilliant idea."

They got to their feet, both of them moving a little stiffly. Picking their way carefully to the edge of the pool, she stripped off and eased herself into the blissful heat.

"Tomorrow morning. Any thoughts on how we're going to handle the SCUMBAGs?"

He didn't answer until he was submerged to the neck. "With extreme prejudice."

"I figured that much. I was hoping for more details, mister I-used-to-be-a-FUC-agent."

He shrugged and reclined until he was more or less floating, one hand gripping the rocks to keep his head above the water. The moon was rising, and there was enough light for her to catch tantalizing glimpses of his gorgeous body just beneath the surface.

"I'm not sure yet, but I'm working on it. A lot will depend on when and where we cross paths. If the universe is feeling generous, we might not run into them at all."

She snorted. "What are the odds of that happening?"

"About as likely as me going vegan." He watched the sky for a long, silent moment. "We're getting out of here, Tabi. No matter what, I'm taking you home tomorrow."

She moved to his side, curling one arm beneath his head and bending down to kiss him. "I'm going to hold you to that."

SUSAN HAYES

He stared up at her, the moonlight making his pale eyes glow. "Say it with me. We're going home tomorrow. Together."

"We're going home tomorrow." She kissed him again before whispering. "Together."

He had her in his arms a second later, a god rising from the steaming water clad only in moonlight and shadow. "Damn right we are."

He made love to her standing in the middle of the pool, and again once they were inside the shelter. He took her with bruising passion, neither of them speaking a word as they came together. It was more than sex and the sharing of their bodies. This was wild, and primal, and as she finally fell asleep, she felt like they were connected on levels she hadn't known existed.

If she hadn't been so exhausted, that would have terrified her. She wasn't falling for Sergei anymore. She'd already fallen, and she still couldn't think of a way for them to be together. She was going into hiding, and she could never ask him to go with her. Hiding wasn't in his nature.

17

Sergei crouched behind a patch of scrubby bushes and cursed. The universe was not feeling generous this morning. In fact, it was clearly in a shit mood. He'd hoped to start while it was still dark and navigate by the stars until there was light enough to see, but that plan had died the moment he'd looked outside their little shelter. The weather had turned foul overnight, blanketing everything in a pall of thick, dark cloud. Between that and the gusts of wet snow that filled the air, they were navigating more by instinct and hope than by the landmarks he'd been able to see so easily yesterday.

If that wasn't bad enough, now they had a new problem to deal with. Unwanted company. He glowered at the man they could barely make out in the early morning light. He was patrolling the trail they needed to follow. Without landmarks, they had to risk it, but the fucking mercs had come to the same conclusion and were apparently waiting for them. He and Tabi were both channelling just enough of their animal forms to have increased speed and agility, but even so, they were racing the clock. Dealing with this guy was going to cost them precious time.

Tabi tugged at his sleeve. When she had his attention, she leaned in and breathed a few careful words in his ear. "Only one of them. Trap, or stupid?"

She had the instincts of an agent. He held up two fingers to indicate he thought it was the second option. He couldn't detect anyone else nearby, and when she nodded in agreement, he knew she thought he was alone, too.

She whispered again, and despite the situation he couldn't help but be turned on by the way her breath caressed his skin. "I distract. You take him down?"

That was a good idea, but he hated it. Distracting the merc meant putting Tabi in danger. He shook his head, and to his surprise, she rolled her eyes at him and raised her hands in a clear message of 'Do you have a better idea?'

Much to his chagrin, he didn't. He shrugged, then pulled his hunting knife out of its sheath, and made several gestures indicating he wanted her to move down the trail before revealing herself so he could come up behind their target while he was distracted. He had to go through it again, because the first time Tabi's eyes were on the knife, not him. He didn't blame her, but there was no other way. Leaving the enemy alive and at their backs was a good way to wind up dead.

He tapped his watch and flashed her two fingers again. Two minutes for them to both get into position.

She nodded, squeezed his hand hard for a second, and

then she was gone, fading into the forest without a sound. She might not believe she was cut out for a life of adventure, but he knew better. She'd been born for this. Now all he had to do was help her see that.

The two minutes he'd given her stretched out like an eternity, giving him time think. He'd been doing a lot of that since last night. Making plans for today, but also thinking about what would happen after they got out of here. He'd meant what he'd said to Tabi. He would get them both home, but he hadn't just been talking about the academy. For the first time in his life, he wanted more than a place to crash between adventures. He wanted something permanent. The more he thought about it, the more certain he was that it was the right choice.

Bast in a wicker fucking basket, is this was maturity felt like?

At two minutes and two seconds, Tabi stepped out of the woods. Her eyes were downcast, her shoulders hunched, her hands raised. "I give up. I'm cold, tired, and exhausted. I just want this nightmare over with."

The merc spun to face her. "Where's the tiger?"

Tabi's face screwed up, and she looked like she was on the point of tears. "He left me behind. Said I was slowing him down and wasn't worth the trouble."

The man raised his gun partway, then held position. "He won't get far. We're covering every inch of this trail."

Liar. There were only a few of them left, and if they were stretched out along the trail, they were leaving a lot of open ground.

Tabi sniffled. "Then I guess it's a good thing I found

this trail, or I'd have frozen to death out there in the woods."

"Which way did he go?"

She pointed in the opposite direction to their goal. "That way. He said with all of you looking for me out here, it would be an easy run back to the parking lot."

"Son of a…" He gestured with the muzzle of his rifle. "Sit your ass down and don't try anything. I need to tell the others."

Sergei was about to make his move, but he stopped when the other man tried to keep his gun trained on Tabi while fumbling one-handed with his radio. Like everything else he had on him, it was military surplus and had seen better days. Probably during World War I. That wasn't his biggest concern, though. Tabi was. The idiot had no concept of firearms safety and could drop Tabi with a tranq dart any second, the way he was fumbling around. As much as they needed the merc to make that call and send the others on a wild goose chase, he couldn't risk her getting hurt.

He took a step out of the bush. Tabi's expression didn't change, but she reached up to scratch the back of her neck, flashing him a subtle signal to wait as she sank to the ground. The move took her out of range of the merc's weapon. *Clever girl.*

He froze, waited a heartbeat, and melted back into the bushes.

Finally, the merc got himself sorted. "This is Hottie. Primary target acquired."

"For fuck's sake, none of us are going to call you that,

so quit trying, Scottie. I didn't hear any gunfire, so how the hell did you acquire her?"

"She surrendered. She's in rough shape, cold, tired, and scared. The tiger bugged out and left her. He's on his way back to the parking lot."

"Fuck! The client wants them both. They're willing to triple our fee for 'em. You stay put and guard the primary. We'll go after the fucking cat."

"Roger that. Good hunting."

Sergei stepped in behind the other man and slashed his throat the moment his finger was off the talk button.

The merc went down with a surprised gurgle, dropping both the gun and his radio as he clutched at the wound in his neck. He'd be dead in seconds.

Sergei grabbed both dropped items, tossed them both to Tabi, then grabbed the still form of the mercenary and dragged him off the path.

"Do what you can to hide the bloodstains, would you?"

"On it." Tabi scrambled to her feet and started kicking fresh snow over the gore. If it kept snowing, there was a chance the other mercs would miss it. Not a great chance, but they didn't have time for more elaborate measures.

He used snow and the dead man's sleeve to remove the blood from his hands, then did a quick search of the corpse, looking for anything that might help FUC identify him later. Proving once again that they had to be bottom of the barrel mercs, he found the man's wallet and ID in an inside pocket of his jacket. *Amateurs.*

The merc had another rifle stashed in his gear. It was an automatic, and his blood ran cold as he recalled yesterday's firefight. The tranqs had been for Tabi. The rest of those shots had been intended to kill. If Joshua and the others hadn't turned back, or if Annie and Danny hadn't been fast enough getting away, someone might have died.

He rejoined Tabi, who had finished doing what she could to hide the evidence of their attack. She held the gun awkwardly, though she kept the muzzle pointed at the ground and her finger far from the trigger, which was more than the former owner had managed.

"I'll take that. Can you monitor the radio? Volume low so it doesn't give them away, but I'd like to keep tabs on them while we run."

"Already on it." She tapped the radio, which she'd managed to clip to the strap of her pack, close to her ear.

"Smart *and* sexy." He checked the rifle, reactivated the safety, and pulled Tabi in for a quick kiss. It was all the reassurance they had time for, but later he planned on a thorough debriefing of everything they'd gone through today. He'd start by debriefing her of her panties and tumbling her into a warm, soft bed that neither of them would leave for at least a day, possibly two. If the academy cafeteria didn't have room service yet they would soon. All he needed was a hot shower, a big bed, steak on demand, and Tabi.

The next hour passed in surreal silence broken only by the occasional outburst from the radio or a curse when one of them tripped over something hidden beneath the snow. At least the storm had passed, the sky clearing by degrees so they had both light and landmarks to navigate by. They'd stayed off the trail at first, but the radio had kept them updated to their enemies' positions, and as soon as they passed the last mercenary they'd moved to the trail. The fresh snow slowed them some, but they were running hard and only a few minutes away from the rendezvous site.

They were going to make it.

That's when he heard it - the unmistakable sound of an approaching helicopter. He turned to her and beamed. "The cavalry is coming!"

"Oh, good." She was breathing so hard she could barely speak. "I would hate to have done all this running for nothing."

"Isn't your father a thoroughbred? I thought they were all about running?"

"On a nice, smooth track for maybe two kilometres, tops." She waved a hand at the trail. "Not hell-bent for leather across a mountainside in winter."

The radio exploded into a cacophony of swearing. "Fuck! Is that a chopper?"

More swearing, and confirmation the others heard it, too.

"Scott. You hearing this? Is it coming your way?" The one he assumed was the merc's leader demanded over the radio. When no one replied, the voice returned. "Fine! Hottie, report. Can you hear the copter? Do you still have eyes on the primary target?"

Shit. Hottie was a rapidly cooling corpse hidden in the woods and wouldn't be answering unless today was the start of the zombie apocalypse.

"Uh oh. Time for more cardio." She groaned and broke

into a run. "When we get back, I'm going to bed for a week!"

"It's a date." He caught up in two strides, grabbing her hand as he passed and pulling her along with him.

They bolted up the steep trail like every demon in hell was on their trail, bursting into the clearing only a few seconds before their ride appeared. The helicopter was so low it was almost skimming the treetops, swooping into the large open space like a hawk. Agents in full tactical gear spilled out the doors before they had even touched down, and within seconds they were surrounded in the middle of a veritable army of well-armed FUC agents.

"Hey there! I heard you needed some help busting MUFF ass." Miranda, legendary FUC agent, lover of carrot cake, and the scariest shifter Sergei had ever met, bounced into view in front of them.

"I was wrong. Not MUFF. They're SCUMBAGs, and they were hired to re-capture Tabitha. What's left of their group is headed this way, including their leader."

"Are the cadets alright? Danny? Annie? They made it back in one piece, didn't they?" Tabi asked.

"They're all fine," Miranda informed her with a smile.

He unclipped the radio from Tabi's pack and handed it to Miranda. "We took this off one of the bodies. They're armed with tranq guns and automatic rifles." He handed over both weapons to her. "If your people could bring one back alive, that would be great. We need to find out who the fuck is after Tabi, and why they've eluded FUC so far."

Miranda just laughed. "Once an agent, always an agent. You sure you don't want to sign back up?"

"Positive. I've already got a career, and it comes with better dental."

"Yeah, but you don't get to say shit like this..." She raised her voice. "Come on, guys. Today, we're hunting SCUMBAGs!"

A few seconds later, the only ones left in the clearing were the two of them, a single, well-armed guard, and the chopper pilot.

Tabi frowned, her gaze moving from him to the trees where Miranda and the other agents had disappeared. "Aren't you going with them?"

It was time to make something clear to his little gothicus. He pulled her into his arms and kissed her hard, his mouth claiming hers as he crushed her against his chest. He didn't let up until his chest burned and the guard cleared his throat so loudly they could hear it over the roar of the copter's rotors. "Why would I want to leave with them, when I can go home with you?"

18

The helicopter was a beast straight out of a Hollywood movie, complete with sliding side doors, a menacing black paint job, and very little in the way of creature comforts. Tabi didn't care. She hunched against the downdraft from the copter's massive blades and clambered inside, wind-blown and almost deafened by the noise.

She waved to the pilot, then made a bee-line for the narrow bench at the back.

She didn't take more than two steps before Sergei hopped in, picked her up, and dropped down on the bench with her in his lap. The engine noise was too loud for her to argue, and when she wriggled, he just smirked and winked at her.

When the guard came on board, he handed them a pair of headsets. Once she got it on, they cut out the worst of the sonic assault, and Sergei showed her how to use the mic so they could talk.

She was still figuring it out when the helicopter took

to the air, and she yelped in confusion and surprise. "Why are we taking off? What about the others?"

The pilot glanced back at them. "Orders, ma'am. We need to get you back to the academy ASAP. Director Cooper was very clear about that."

"But the agents?"

"We'll come back for them." And with that, the pilot and guard lapsed into silence, leaving them alone.

It was noisy, and the ride was far from smooth, but she didn't pay much attention. She was trying to focus on Sergei, memorizing every detail. Once they touched down, things would happen fast. There'd be debriefings and discussions, and if FUC couldn't figure out who was behind the attempted abduction, she'd have to go into hiding.

Leaving him was going to hurt so much. She buried her face in his shoulder so he wouldn't see her cry, but after a few seconds he stroked her cheek, wiping away her tears with a calloused finger tip.

"What's wrong?"

"I don't know if I'll ever see you again."

He blinked at her. "Of course you are. Why the hell wouldn't you?"

She looked up at him with red, swollen eyes. "Because I'm not cut out for a life of adventure. I wanted to be, but I'm not. And that's the kind of woman you need. Plus, I need to hide for a while, and we both know running and hiding isn't your style."

He chuckled, the sound almost lost in the din of the engine noise, but she felt the comforting rumble from

SUSAN HAYES

deep inside his chest. "Bullshit. From where I'm sitting, you and I just survived an epic adventure."

"No, we ran from a group of assholes who wanted to put us in cages. It wasn't an adventure, it was a nightmare."

"Ah." He wiped her tears from her cheeks and cuddled her closer. "I see the problem. I've got news for you, sweetheart. Every grand saga and exploit you've ever heard was a fucking nightmare to the ones experiencing it. I think it's like childbirth. At the time it's happening, it's all pain, screaming, and solemn vows to never do it again. After it's all over, we gloss over those bits. Time passes, the memory fades, and we end up going off to find trouble all over again."

She shook her head. "I'm never going to want to find this kind of trouble again."

"Care to make a bet on that?" His cocky smile was almost enough to make her laugh.

"You really think so?"

"I do."

"And what if I have to disappear for a while?"

He kissed the tip of her nose. "Don't borrow trouble. We'll burn that bridge when we come to it."

"Right." Some of the sadness left her, and the tight bands around her chest loosened up enough that she could breathe easier. She laid her head on Sergei's shoulder and closed her eyes, just for a few seconds.

146

She woke up when they landed, the bump shaking her awake. How the hell had she fallen asleep in all that noise?

"Cat naps are the best naps," Sergei declared as he yawned and stretched.

"You, too?" If Sergei had also been asleep, she could stop feeling like the weakest link.

"Out like a light," he admitted without a trace of shame. Then he stood with her still in his arms and made for the door.

"I can walk."

"Yes, you can."

"I mean right now. Put me down."

"I think we've had this conversation before. Remind me, how did that go for you?"

She huffed. "You got bossy and wouldn't listen."

"Yeah. That's kind of my thing. I thought you'd realized that by now."

"So, you're not putting me down?"

He grinned, tightened his grip on her, and jumped from the chopper to the ground with an annoying amount of grace and style. "Nope."

"Stubborn cat."

"Glorious gothicus. Smile, we have company."

She'd been focused on their conversation and hadn't paid attention to anything else, like the gathering of cadets, instructors, and staff waiting for them on the snow-streaked lawn. As she looked up in shock, they started to cheer, led by the distinctive figure of the Director herself. By her side were some familiar faces: Annie, Danny, Pete, and Janice.

Relief hit her hard. Miranda had said they were all okay, but now she could see for herself.

"You made it!" Annie rushed forward. "We've been so worried."

"Indeed we have." Alyce shot the overeager bear an imperious look, and Annie took a quick step back. "Anything I need to know?"

Sergei didn't answer the question. Instead, he asked two of his own. "Did Miranda and the others find the mercs? Who are they working for?"

"Yes, and that's classified," Cooper replied.

Sergei growled. "Then you better find a way to declassify it for Tabi and me, soon."

The director's mouth twitched in the faintest trace of a smile. "I'll take that under advisement. Now, is there anything I should know about?"

"Yeah. They were SCUMBAGs, and they've been watching this place waiting for Tabi to leave. You might want to up your security a bit, Director Cooper. All is not as quiet as it seems, and someone is trying to abduct one of your employees."

Alyce bared her teeth. "Not on my watch. Ms. Willows was the focus of this attack?"

"Yes, ma'am," Tabi interjected. "They kept referring to me as the primary target."

Everyone in earshot quieted at that bit of news.

"You were close enough to hear them talking?"

Sergei raised his voice so everyone could hear him. "Tabi saved my tail out there. If it weren't for her shifting into battle-corn mode, I'd be in a cage somewhere right now."

His words made Tabi blush with embarrassment and pride.

"Battle-corn? That's good." Janice nodded. "Way better than Stab... well, you know."

"I think so, too." She flashed the coyote shifter a grateful smile. "How are Joshua and Guy?"

Janice's lips thinned. "Fully recovered, and no longer attending the academy. I think Josh is actually happy about it. He never really wanted to be an agent. That was his father's idea. Guy..." Janice shrugged. "He's happy to follow Josh wherever."

"But you're staying?"

The girl beamed. "I'm staying."

Director Cooper cleared her throat. "Anything else?"

Tabi shook her head, but Sergei had more to say.

"Just one thing." He raised his voice even louder. "This is a public service announcement. Tabi is my mate. Anyone who has an issue with her, has an issue with me. If she doesn't kick your ass, I will."

Joy and embarrassement went to war inside her head, and after a messy battle, joy won...and was immediately joined by a jolt of outrage as she realized he'd skipped a key step. She poked him in the chest, nearly bruising her finger in the process. "Hey! You haven't asked me yet, you pushy, arrogant feline!"

"Would that change the answer?" he retorted.

"Well, no. But dammit, you should have asked."

Alyce's brows rose almost to her hairline. "So, you'll be leaving us, then, Ms. Willows?"

Once again, Sergei answered before she could. "That's up to Tabi, but I don't think it will be necessary. Director

Cooper, would you still be interested in having a survival trainer on staff?"

"I… well… certainly."

"Great. Then we can talk about my contract tomorrow. I've got a few ideas I want to run by you."

It made her feel marginally better to note that he didn't wait for the director to answer. He swept past *everyone* like a king dismissing his court.

"You're staying? Here?"

"Looks that way."

"When did you decide all this?"

"I've been thinking about it since last night, but honestly, it all sort of came to me just now." As he looked at her, his expression showed a hint of doubt. "If it's okay with you, I mean. And if we have to go into protection for a while, I'm good with that."

"But your show! And I thought you didn't run from things?"

"My show is on hiatus until I figure out how to deal with MUFF, and we still need to figure out who's after you and how to stop it. That might take a while. So, for now, I thought I'd stay here and protect my mate." He grinned. "You know, try a new kind of adventure."

"Won't you get bored?"

"Of this place, maybe. Of you? Never." He stopped walking and kissed her, his mouth hard and demanding as he made love to her mouth with near indecent thoroughness. After a soul searing eternity, he moved his lips a scant distance from hers and whispered. "I love you."

"Oh." She mulled that over for a minute, almost afraid to say yes. He was offering her everything she'd always wanted, including a life with a man she'd dreamed about for years. It would be an adventure all right.

He was at the door to her room before she spoke again, and she could see he was agitated about her continued silence, but dammit, he'd sprung all of this on her, he could just wait a few minutes for her to think it over. "I… I love you too, Sergei. But what if I'm the one who gets bored and wants to do something new with my life? I mean, careerwise, not you." She grinned a little. "You, I think I'll keep."

He carried her inside and kicked the door shut behind them. "Well I'm definitely keeping you, so that's settled. As for what happens if you get bored? Then we'll find something new for us both. I've had plenty of adventures already. I'd like to share some of yours."

He lowered her to the ground, sliding her over every hard inch of his body on the way down, making her brain short circuit for a moment.

"Can you put that in the form of a question, please?" She asked when her mouth reconnected to her brain.

He took her hand and dropped to one knee in front of her, his ice-blue eyes gleaming. "Tabitha Willows, will you join me in a lifetime of adventure?"

Manes and tails, this was really happening. She squeezed his hand and nodded like a bobble-head doll in an earthquake. Her throat was too tight to speak for a few seconds, but eventually, she managed to squeak out a "Yes!"

He was on his feet in a flash, wrapping her in his arms and spinning her around until they were both laughing and breathless.

She had no idea what their future looked like, but that didn't worry her. They were on the first page of a new adventure, the future unwritten except for five little words. They lived happily ever after.

Thank you for reading!

There are more FUC Academy books coming each month!

To find out more about these books and more, visit Worlds.EveLanglais.com or sign up for the EveL Worlds newsletter. If you haven't already downloaded the **free Academy intro** (written by Eve Langlais) make sure you grab it at worlds.evelanglais.com/wordpress/book/fucacademy1!

ABOUT THE AUTHOR

Susan lives out on the Canadian west coast surrounded by open water, dear family and good friends. She has jumped out of perfectly good airplanes on purpose and accidentally swum with sharks on the Great Barrier Reef. If the world ends, she plans to survive as the spunky, comedic sidekick to the heroes of the new world, because she's too damned short and out of shape to make it on her own for long.

Writing is her joy, her escape from reality and the only way she knows of to quiet the nagging harridan of a muse the universe assigned to her.

Social media and other links: